≫ ≫

CASEY FLANAGAN comes to spend the summer in the small southern town where her grandparents live, not knowing a soul her age, shy about making new friends, wishing she could just turn around and go home.

Then she meets Dwayne Pickens. From the very first day, Casey and Dwayne form a special friendship. But Dwayne is a man thirty-three whose mind has never grown beyond that of a boy twelve. He loves baseball, hates girls, and simply assumes Casey—with her short hair and jeans —is the new boy in town. In time, Casey comes to protect Dwayne as she enjoys his easy ways and shares his one big fear of being sent away again to the "home," a place he dreads.

It is a summer of surprises for Casey whose life weaves in and out of the lives of many other people who love her: Jane and Ben Flanagan whose home is a solid comfortable place; the wreckless Taylor Flanagan, her stock-car racer uncle, who draws Casey into the center of things; Hazard Whitaker, the middle-aged loveable loser his name typifies; Pansy, the prim but warm-hearted spinster whose courtship with Hazard is awkward, loving and irresistible to Casey and all those who watch it unfold.

Casey affects these people indelibly, and cannot help being affected in turn, especially by Dwayne who is unforgettable to her. Dwayne's happiness is infectious, but his vulnerability leads to a disaster that pulls Casey, her family, and the community together in an unselfish act to save him.

In a remarkable way, Sue Ellen Bridgers' new novel is a sensitive portrayal of a girl approaching adolescence, as well as a heartfelt story of a community. Her ability to show simple, innocent people doing what they have to do with courage and foolishness and love and pain is unparalleled. By defying categorization, *All Together Now* is a hopeful story for everyone, a book to be long remembered.

All Together Now

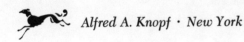 **A NOVEL**

Sue Ellen Bridgers

Alfred A. Knopf · New York

THIS IS A BORZOI BOOK PUBLISHED BY ALFRED A. KNOPF, INC.

Manufactured in the United States of America 10 9 8 7 6 5 4 3 2 1
Library of Congress Cataloging in Publication Data.   Bridgers, Sue Ellen. All together now. Summary: Casey spends her twelfth summer visiting her grand-parents in their small town while her father serves in the Korean War and her mother works two jobs. [1. Grandparents—Fiction] I. Title.
PZ7.B7615Al 1979 [Fic] 78–12244 ISBN 0–394–84098–4
ISBN 0–394–94098–9 lib. bdg.

J
B

➔ ➔ *For*
Elizabeth
Jane
Sean
in exchange for smiles

ꙍꙍ *All Together Now*

∗ *1* ∗

Casey came unwill-
ingly. So, when the bus pulled into the station after
six hours of farmland, sky, and trees seen through the
gray tinted glass that made everything look artificial,
she sat still while the people around her got up, stretching, sighing, lifting down packages from above their
heads. She sat there, hands folded in her lap, unable
to look out the window, unable to reconcile herself to
a summer away from home even though she knew
that when she did look, a familiar face would be there
to greet her.

Perhaps her grandfather with his summer hat pushed
back on his balding head, rimless glasses slipped beneath the hump of his thin nose. Maybe her grandmother in her black lace-up Sunday shoes, her pocketbook like a weapon at her side, her hand raised against
the sun in her eyes. Or Taylor, off the job for a few
minutes to deliver his niece home, in shirt sleeves and
with pants bagging at the knees, grinning at her, his
hand out to pull her off the roaring bus like a knight
rescuing a lady from a belching dragon.

It was her grandmother. Jane Flanagan stood there
with her hand shading her eyes, the solitary welcomer
in the empty bus station, waiting for a granddaughter

who would be her child for the summer because her real child, Casey's father, was off in Korea fighting his second war.

Jane waited for a child's face, a girl's face, to appear at the window and look down at her as the bus spewed exhaust on the splotched concrete. But there was no face. The bus shuddered, growled, died. The door opened, and passengers started out. Moses from down the street, back from visiting his sister; the Farmer girls, home from a shopping trip; two strangers.

Her heart rose just like it had when she'd heard her mother was dead twenty-two years ago, just like it had when the lumberyard burned in 1938 and she hadn't known for hours if her husband and son were safe. Like it did when she knew David would be flying in yet another war. Her heart rose, pushing in her chest, cutting off her breath. And then a head appeared, tiny it seemed to her, like an infant's head, smooth with short shiny brown hair. A cheek, a profile that made her heart stop, then two eyes turning toward her hesitantly. David's eyes. Deep set, wrapped in shadows of their own making. Her husband's eyes, her son's.

My goodness, she's shy, Jane thought, opening her arms. That's the difference between eleven and twelve, between Christmas and summertime. Long legs and arms, gangliness, a face turned away from kisses.

She was wearing pants, too. Long pants to hide in, as if dresses exposed too much. A boy's shirt opened at the neck. And saddle oxfords that looked the size of Taylor's.

It was a mistake to call her Casey, Jane thought as she held the thin body close to her. She knew that only she held on; Casey merely stood in her embrace resolutely, doing her duty. It's too much a boy's name, Jane said to herself.

"Sweetheart, I'm so glad you're here at last! I almost had a fright when you weren't the first one off the bus!" She turned the girl away from her but kept her arm about her.

"I have to get my suitcase," Casey said uneasily.

"Of course you do," her grandmother said. "What am I thinking? The truth is, Casey, I'm not at all accustomed to meeting buses. Usually I send your grandpa or Taylor on errands like this. But then there's never anyone quite so important to meet as a granddaughter coming by herself all the way from South Carolina." Jane hugged Casey again while the driver unloaded the baggage. "Which one is yours, honey? Can you carry that big old thing all the way home? Why, goodness gracious, it weighs a ton! I should have brought the car, but it's such a nice day and I thought you'd like to stretch your legs a little." Jane pretended to tug at the suitcase.

"I can carry it," Casey said.

And with the suitcase banging against her leg, they went down the walk toward the edge of town and the tree-shaded street where the Flanagans had always lived. Her grandmother talked on and on about how glad they were she had come and how her grandfather and Taylor would be home at suppertime.

Casey watched the street silently, looking for familiar signs, a tree she remembered, a house she'd once visited in, some obvious signal that she should be here at all. The houses were large and looming and very quiet at mid-afternoon. She wished she hadn't come.

The wish almost brought tears to her eyes when she remembered how, at home, she'd be in the club pool right now or riding her bike to her best friend's house, where they'd eat ice cream off sticks and catch bees in pint jars or make clover chains.

She could see the edge of the Flanagans' yard and then the walk curving up to the porch, familiar but not dear to her. It wasn't her house.

"Well, we're almost home," Jane said as if she knew what Casey's silence meant.

Just then Casey heard a noise, a metallic ring, the thump of something hard and solid striking metal, the pounding of dirt, and then the voice, an announcer's voice, singsonging a mental picture she could not yet visualize.

"What's that?" She stopped to peer through the trees on the other side of the street, searching out the source of the chatter. The metallic clatter echoed again. A long swish—somebody sliding—a dusty voice sputtering.

"That's Dwayne Pickens, playing ball," Jane said, walking on.

"Who's he playing with? Is he new? I don't know Dwayne Pickens, do I?" Casey asked, heartened by the prospect of another kid in this neighborhood of ancient houses and, it seemed to her, even older occupants.

"Of course you don't. He just moved here. Dora Pickens and her family lived for years and years over on Plum. Dr. Pickens was a fine man, a good dentist, too, but he died a few years ago, not long after their other children were married. One of them lives in the big house on Plum now. Dora didn't see much point in keeping such a big place for her and Dwayne, so she bought that little house across the street from us a year ago. It's small, but there's an empty lot with it and a garage for Dwayne." Jane sighed.

"As for Dwayne," she continued, "he's in his thirties, your daddy's age, but he's got the mind of a twelve-year-old. Retarded but harmless. He likes baseball and toys just like a boy would. He goes all over town on his own. Everybody knows him so he never gets into any real trouble. Once, though, a while back, they sent him off to a home, an institution I reckon it was, but Dora got him back as soon as she could. She's a saint, but he's a burden on her any way you look at it. Makes me thank God every day my two boys were born healthy and right in the head." Jane turned up her walk, leaving Casey on the sidewalk.

Through the thin line of trees she could see a figure on the dusty vacant lot. He stood in the middle of the field, slightly elevated on what must be the pitcher's mound. He was adjusting his black cap over his eyes.

"Reese steps into the box, ready to see what Dickson will give him this time. Pee Wee's oh-for-three so far today. He's flied to left, walked, and grounded to third," he yelled to his invisible audience.

Casey could see the yellow baseball in his hand as he flipped it with short snaps of his wrist. He looked hard toward the plate, set the arch of his right foot firmly across the rubber, and swung both hands behind himself while sliding his left leg back and dropping his head down. Then he swung both hands high over his head, where they met and were hidden somewhere behind his black cap. He pushed off with his left foot onto his right, swung his left leg into the air in front of him, dropped his right arm behind his back while balancing his left hand high in the air, swung his glove down, and followed it in a windmill motion with the right hand.

"Here's the windup and the pitch!"

The ball flew high toward the plate, then darted to the left and dropped suddenly across the outside edge of the plate. It whammed into the bottom half of the empty oil drum behind the plate and bounced back sharply between first and second base.

"It's a curve! Pee Wee swings and hits a hard ground ball toward second!"

Balanced on his toes like a diver, his right arm still across his chest in the follow-through, the man sprang to the left after the bouncing ball, then threw himself headlong at it.

"And Basgall can't get it! Pee Wee rounds first and holds up there for a single!" he shouted from the ground.

"What's he doing?" Casey asked her grandmother, who was waiting for her halfway up the walk.

"I told you, honey, he's playing baseball."

"By himself?"

"Does it look like he needs anybody else? He's got the Dodgers and the Pirates already." Jane came back to where Casey was standing. Together they watched as Dwayne picked himself up off the ground and trotted out into right field after the ball. Reaching down, he flipped the ball up into the webbing of his glove, tossed it into the air, and caught it in his bare hand. He was grinning when he walked back to the pitcher's mound.

"Hey boy, atta way to go, boy!" he called.

Jane stood watching him through the trees as if he

were something from another time, something dear and familiar and yet lost to her. "Do you ever go out by yourself, Casey, maybe to sit in a tree or on the porch swing or just to wander around, and out there, all by yourself, things happen to you? You imagine wonderful, exciting times. You dream in your head with your eyes wide open till you forget it isn't real. Well, Dwayne's like that, except he doesn't know enough to keep his dreaming quiet. He doesn't see people laughing at him. Or maybe he doesn't care. He's gullible, you see, and more honest than most of us."

"Maybe he'll let me play with him," Casey said almost to herself. "I could run the bases."

"I doubt it," Jane said, hoping to squelch any such notions before they had time to settle. "He's like a twelve-year-old boy, you remember. He won't have anything to do with girls. Besides, there're plenty of young people around for you. Not that I object to Dwayne. He's respectful and good-natured. But still . . ." Her voice trailed off, not knowing what else to say.

Run the bases, she was thinking. No matter how she tried, there seemed little hope of having a girl in her house. Two sons and now a granddaughter in pants and saddle oxfords who wanted to play baseball with Dwayne Pickens.

"Let's get you settled," she said to Casey, who was finally following her around the house to the kitchen door. "I thought you'd like to have your daddy's room. Oh, Casey, we had the nicest letter from him yesterday. I'll let you read it. Of course, he doesn't know you've come for the summer yet. We'll have to write him all about it. I know it'll make him feel better. You know, he seems so close when a letter comes, like he's right down there in South Carolina and not all the way in Korea. Who'd have thought there'd be another war, Casey?" They pushed through the screen door and stood in the middle of the kitchen. "Who'd have thought there wasn't enough learning done the last time?" She sighed, conjuring up memories of sad times, of Dwayne Pickens and her David growing up together and then leaving each other—at twelve, one mind slipped past the other—and now her David at war while Dwayne pitched baseballs at an oil drum.

"Well, let's get cheerful," she said suddenly. "A merry heart, you know. A happy house." She stopped short and let out a soft, round chuckle. "And just look who's coming!"

❧ 2 ❧

*L*ooks like *we're going* to have a full house. A hat on every hook," she said, surmising her situation with a smile, "because here comes Hazard!"

They were standing in the kitchen, the woman in her straw summer hat and the girl with her hand still on her suitcase, as if she were trying to decide whether to go or to stay. They froze there like a painted audience before a make-believe show, the screen door making a gray haze between them and the awaited attraction.

Having reached the porch, the man called Hazard leaned forward on his toes, ready to knock.

"Sh-h-h-h," Grandmother whispered, and Casey released her fingers slowly from the handle of her bag.

"*Rap-p-p-p!*" One solid blow crashed against the door jamb and then they watched through the screen as the man sprinted off the steps and bent down to scoop up a handful of dry dirt from the flower bed below. Back on the porch, he shook the dirt onto the glossy painted floor to make it crunch under his feet, and took off his hat, which he held to his chest as if acknowledging the flag.

Casey looked from the apparition on the porch to her grandmother, who showed no sign of surprise. She was smiling like someone who knew the punch line but wanted to hear the joke anyway.

"What you doing out there, Hazard?" she called as if she were a great distance from him.

"You come on out here, Jane!" the man shouted back. "You come on, now!"

Grandmother put her black patent pocketbook on the kitchen table and began slapping her thighs in response to some music in her head. Her bosom heaved happily to the alternating rhythm of her hands and the foot she had begun to pat on the hardwood floor.

"Hazard, Hazard, where you been?" she called out.

"Down the track and I'm going again!" the man sang back.

"What you gonna do when you get back?"

"Come in your house and hit the sack!"

Rhythm established and attention drawn, the man began to dance. The dirt crunched under his cheap wing-tips as he shuffled across the porch, hat flailing in his swinging hand. His torso, straining at shoulder and elbow against his ill-fitting blue plaid jacket, seemed confined, almost motionless, while his long thin arms balanced his agile legs between the screen door and the pots of geraniums that lined the porch railing. He seemed lighter than Casey could imagine a man being. And yet there was a kind of desperation in his movements, as if he felt he had put himself against impossible odds and must prove himself again. He whirled on his feet, slapped his hat against his thigh, and shook the other hand in the air as he did a kick step across the porch.

"Hazard, watch out!" Jane called.

But it was too late. The man's long white fingers,

spread wide and shaking, had collided with the first of the geranium pots, which in turn toppled onto the next one. Both pots leaned askew for a second and then fell over the railing into the dirt.

"G-D, I broke my hand!" he yelled, holding the injury to his chest and massaging it frantically with the other hand. "Get some soaking water! Get a splint! Get a doctor!"

Jane was smiling. "That's Hazard," she said to Casey. "His hand's not broken, but he knows my clay pots are."

"Just offering a little entertainment," Hazard was muttering, having noted that aid was not forthcoming. "Just getting off on the right foot." He cackled suddenly, his face mobile and bright. "You hear that, Jane?" he yelled through the screen. "Off on the right foot! Hah, hah, hah!"

Grandmother went to the door and swung it open, as if the man were just arriving and her geraniums were where they were supposed to be.

"Hazard, welcome home," she said and let out a gigantic happy sigh. She was smiling with unabashed pleasure.

"That's right kind of you, Miss Jane," the man said. He dropped his injured hand to his side as though he had no further need of it and bent himself through the door jamb although he was less than six feet tall. He seemed to stoop unconsciously, as if he'd spent many years getting into places that proved uncomfortable to him.

"Why, you've already got company," he complained, seeing Casey, who still stood beside her suitcase. He paused to look her up and down. "Great God, it's David's little girl, ain't it?" He was glad to see she was somebody he knew. He could feel like one of the family as long as there weren't other outsiders around to remind him that he, like they, wasn't blood kin to the Flanagans.

"Of course it's Casey, but I'm surprised you recognized her," Jane Flanagan said, putting her arm around her granddaughter. "She's twelve years old this past spring. All grown up."

"Don't believe it," Hazard boomed. "I don't believe it! Twelve, you say! Great God, and I'm just thirty-five myself. Just hitting my prime!"

"He can't even remember when he last saw thirty-five," Jane said to Casey. "Why, when your Uncle Taylor turns thirty-five, Hazard won't even recognize it on him, it's been so long since he's seen thirty-five."

"Listen to her! What did I come here for? To get talked about?" Hazard slouched into a kitchen chair trying to look dejected. "Here I am with this injured hand paining me something terrible, and this woman goes on, poking fun, taking advantage of my mistaking my age. Never was good at numbers. That's why I never made any money, girl. The only reason. I knew I wouldn't appreciate it like other folks. Didn't want to figure on it. Didn't want to count it. Five dollars. Now there's a good amount. Simple to figure on. Don't bulge in your wallet. You can set down on it easy. Nobody's gonna rob you for it, but it'll get you a place to sleep and some rat cheese to nibble on any day you're needing it."

"I reckon that means you're hungry," Jane said. "Everybody in this house eats at twelve sharp, in case you don't remember. But"—she smiled at him—"considering that Casey here just got off the bus from Fort

Jackson, South Carolina, and it's three good hours till suppertime, I suppose I could get you both something. Something cold, mind you, Hazard. Something cold and left over."

"Her leftovers are perfection," Hazard said to Casey, pulling out a chair for her with his injured hand. "Her leftovers are fit for kings. Her—"

"Her leftovers are just that." Jane put plates in front of them. "Casey, don't you mind him. He's always thought he had to flatter me. Goes on and on with this foolishness like I was paying attention to him. I don't pay you any mind, Hazard." She put a plate of sliced ham on the table, followed by potato salad and sliced cucumbers soaking in vinegar.

Hazard attacked the food like it was a foe to be reckoned with. Casey cut and chewed carefully, watching her manners and the man at the same time. She'd heard about Hazard all her life, so his performance on the porch didn't surprise her much. She was grateful he'd come, though. Here was somebody who would eagerly draw attention to himself, filling her grandmother's time with his antics so that Casey could slip away unnoticed and be by herself. Not that she wanted to be alone all the time, but she didn't want her grandmother hovering over her, either, like she was an orphan or a charity case. What she wanted was to be doing something, not talking about it.

After lunch she slipped out the back door, passed the broken geraniums, and went around the house toward the vacant lot where she'd seen Dwayne Pickens. Crossing the street toward the trees in the Pickenses' yard, she wondered vaguely if she should have asked her grandmother's permission, or at least told her where she was going. She wasn't used to telling anyone where she was going at home. With both parents working, she had learned early what would do and what wouldn't, and she enjoyed both her independence and her parents' confidence in her. Besides, being around so many people in uniform had given her a special, if misplaced, sense of safety. It was like meeting a policeman on every corner. You never expected to be hit on the head midway the block.

She heard the ball hit the metal drum.

"And here's the pitch. Robinson *bunts!* Holy cow!"

Dwayne dashed to the plate, picked up the ball with his bare hand, turned and made a throwing motion toward first base, although he still held the ball in his hand. He raced off toward first himself.

"Garagiola's off with the mask! He grabs the ball and fires it to first! Is it in time?"

At first base, Dwayne toed the bag and then snared the ball from its invisible flight with a flick of his gloved wrist.

"They've got him. Garagiola throws out Robinson on a beau-ti-ful play! And that's all for the Dodgers! In the top of the ninth, it's three up and three down!"

Casey was at the fence now. She wrapped her fingers around the wire and leaned into it for a better look. The man was on his way back to the mound. He was wearing khaki work pants and a T-shirt to which dirt clung in sweaty patches. He was short, although still a head taller than Casey, and his body was hard and muscular. Casey tried to make out his face from under the bill of his cap, but she could see only his chin and cheeks, a rugged jaw without a hint of the weakness she'd expected him to expose.

It must be in his eyes, she thought. That's where his stupid look must be.

But just then he took off his cap to wipe his forehead with the back of his head. She saw a full head of thick dark hair, a wide clear forehead, and then the eyes. She couldn't see their color, but even from that distance she knew they weren't wild.

He knocked his cleats on the mound and moved a wad of tobacco to his cheek, then sent a squirt of brown juice straight in front of him, right toward her.

"Hey boy," he called in a voice more gruff than his announcer's tone, but just as loud. "Whatcha doin' here, boy?"

Casey felt her stomach lurch. She loosened her fingers from the wire and moved back a step.

"Hey boy! Hey you! Whatcha doin'?" Dwayne was coming toward her, trotting like players do when they're heading for the dugout.

"Just looking," Casey said, still backing away. The gate to the fence was farther down, but she knew he could jump the chicken wire to get to her if he wanted to.

He stopped, leaned into the same spot where she'd stood, and looked out from beneath his cap at her.

"I've come to stay with my grandparents," she said, desperate not to show fear in her voice. It's like talking to an animal, she thought. I can't let him know I'm scared. "You know the Flanagans across the street, don't you?" Surely he knew and liked them. He'd been her father's friend years ago. Or could he remember after all these years of being twelve?

"Miss Jane?" He began to grin. "I like that lady. One time a boy, he come by here and pitched to me. I hit one clean across the street right up on Miss Jane's porch. Boy, I can tell you I was scared! How about if I broke something? What would Mama say? And Alva? You know my brother Alva? He gets so mad at me! Really *mad!* Anyhow, 'nothing broken.' That's what your grandma says to me. She says, 'It's all right, Dwayne Pickens. And you come see me sometime.' " He was beaming at her, having remembered the conversation so vividly that it gave him pleasure again. "I like that woman."

Now she looked right into his eyes. They were gray eyes, and although he squinted against the sunlight at her, Casey could see that they were clear, unshadowed by his slow-moving brain. He didn't look retarded at all. Only his speech betrayed his childishness, for he slurred over words, bobbing his head as if to help himself think.

"What's your name?" he was saying. "Hey boy, what's your name?"

Casey moved a step closer to him and took a deep breath. She had never done what she was now thinking to do. She had never lied, at least not a big lie, a gigantic lie, one that could change her summer. Yet the proportions of her dishonesty didn't scare her, for it seemed right, both for her and for Dwayne Pickens, that she should say the words that could give them both so much pleasure.

"K.C. Flanagan," she said slowly, testing the sound she made. "K.C.—I'm David Flanagan's kid. I'm spending the summer right across the street."

"Hot dog!" Dwayne was shaking the fence in his excitement. "You like baseball?"

"Yeah," Casey said, remembering girls' softball games. She knew baseball wasn't all that different.

"What position?" Dwayne wanted to know.

"Most anywhere. Not much of a hitter, though."

"Don't need a hitter," Dwayne said. He moved his tobacco against his cheek and spit on the ground at his feet. "Need a outfielder. Run myself ragged out there. You don't want to pitch, do you? 'Cause I'm the pitcher."

"Never been much on the mound," Casey said, gaining confidence. If she had already convinced Dwayne Pickens that she was a boy, surely she could convince him she knew baseball.

"Casey!" It was her grandmother. "Casey, where are you?"

"That's Miss Jane right there," Dwayne said. "She's a-callin' you for something."

"I got to go," Casey said. "Maybe I'll see you tomorrow."

"Yeah." Dwayne looked a little disappointed that she was leaving so soon. Then he brightened and slapped his cap on his thigh. "Tomorrow we'll go downtown. I can show you everything." His face seemed to expand as he envisioned the sights in store for them. "Maybe we'll go to the show."

"Well, 'bye, Dwayne," Casey said.

" 'Bye."

Casey started across the street to her grandmother.

"Hey boy!" She could hear Dwayne calling. "See you tomorrow, boy!"

"So you met him already," Jane said when Casey reached her.

"Yes," Casey panted, out of breath from excitement as much as from running. "Grandma, he thinks I'm a boy," she said softly.

"Now just how did that happen?" Jane wanted to know. She started down the sidewalk with Casey trotting after her.

"I just didn't say I was a girl," Casey said breathlessly. "Casey could be a boy's name, too, you know. He just never thought any different."

"Not telling him is the same as lying, Casey," Jane said slowly.

"I know, Grandma, but it won't hurt anything. How can it? When school starts I'll be gone. Besides, I don't intend to spend my whole summer with Dwayne Pickens."

"I should hope not." Jane walked on ahead, trying to decide what she should say. If Casey were one of her own boys, she knew what she'd do—send him packing across the street to tell the truth—but this was her grandchild, a little girl with a father fighting a war and her mother at work—an abandoned child was one way of looking at it—who'd come here to have a family. How many more summers would there be for her to enjoy herself? And if she wanted a retarded person for a friend, why should his poor stumbling mind and opinions stop her? "I won't tell Dwayne," Jane said finally.

"Thanks, Grandma," Casey said, and Jane saw her smile for the first time.

3

*H*azard Whitaker lay on the bed in the Flanagans' guest room, his stomach resting easy with Jane's leftovers but his head troubling over the problem he always had when he came for a visit.

Arriving at this house always reminded Hazard of where he'd come from. Which was nowhere. At fifty-two, he was without almost anything that gave a man reason to look back on his life with pride—no wife or children, no home except two rooms above a restaurant, no career, no savings account, no automobile. Lately he'd even been feeling a little embarrassed about his occupation, a fate he'd never expected to come to because he'd always admired entertainers, people who could make others forget their troubles for a while and pat their feet a little. Now he wasn't so proud of being a dancing man.

Of course, he hadn't always been a dancing man. No, years ago when he first met Ben Flanagan in the rail-road station, he'd been a salesman. Selling shoes back then. After that, a fine line of kitchenware. Then what? Borrowed money from Ben to take a three-months' photography course over in Charlotte and came out of there taking group pictures right in your family setting.

He tinted the pictures for two-fifty extra, and most people ordered themselves in color. Vanity took over when people got their pictures made.

But then everybody got a camera. Hazard considered going into the photography equipment business, selling tripods, fancy lenses, and light meters door to door, but he didn't really have his heart in it. People didn't care about taking fine pictures, just quick ones.

So he'd gone looking for his first love, his childhood fantasy—dancing—and had come as close to it as he thought he ever would. He got a job waiting tables. Never one to settle for a single gesture when he could envision two, Hazard spun between the tables at Papa Tutoni's Spaghetti House, twirling dishes and balancing trays with an acrobatic skill that came to him magically when he had an appreciative audience. Almost every Saturday night, Tutoni's cousin would come in to play the piano for tips. Then Hazard could really dance. The old piano would surge with a rumpled, thumping bass as the girl rippled through "Side by Side" and "Carolina in the Morning," and Hazard would start the slow, rocking steps that made heads turn and forks slip onto plates of pasta.

He knew he could dance. Great God, his head went light with the thought of faces turning to him above the blinking candles stuck in bottles. Then he would lose sight of the audience and just be out there alone, free of every worry known to man, while orders backed up in the kitchen and Papa Tutoni slapped his doughy fingers on his apron and lifted his eyes to the dingy ceiling. Who was to know how much business this crazy man brought in? Sure he was good, but so was the lasagne and the ravioli, not to mention the pizza. And

who ever heard of a dancing Italian waiter? Not that
Hazard could pass for an Italian even in the dark. If
he were just an accordion player or a violinist. A singer
even, Papa Tutoni would lament. Anything but a dancing man.

Still, Hazard could make the customers happy. They
ordered more wine, a little dessert, another coffee.
Hazard could stop arguments with his toes, mend
romances with a little shuffle to the left. He could lift
his head, eyes all dreamy, and make a roomful of eyes
lift with him, going outside themselves just like Hazard
was doing, with smiles they'd never recognized on
their own faces.

Now he was in the Flanagans' house, in the room
that had long ago come to be known as his, and he was
staring at the ceiling with his mind on Pansy.

Over the twenty-five years since he'd first brightened
Jane Flanagan's door on the heels of Ben—who'd found
him asleep beside his shoe samples on a train station
bench—he'd spent considerable time wondering what
to do about Jane's best friend, Pansy, for she'd con-
sistently poached on his feelings from the first moment he'd laid eyes on her.

He could remember to this day how she'd looked, her
napkin in her lap, her wrists resting lightly on the table
edge, her voice whispering amidst the clicking of fork
and china plate. She came to supper every Thursday
night. That Hazard learned when the two women had
the dishes done and were finding their jackets to go to
choir practice. It was a ritual of theirs nurtured through
a teen-age friendship, on into the first years of their
adult lives when Ben Flanagan was wooing Jane,
through the newly married years when Jane, seeing

no reason to give up a good and true friend, arranged her young mother's life to include another woman whom folks were still expecting to marry off just any day.

When Hazard saw Pansy coming in from the kitchen that autumn evening, his first thought was of her husband and where he might be. Maybe a traveling man like himself, or a doctor making rounds, or a fireman on duty. Or could it be that he was sick and she, just having touched his forehead with a damp cloth and cool hand, had left him sleeping to come down the street for a decent meal urged on her by a good friend. All this he imagined in an instant, never once thinking that she was as free as he, as able to love as he, as ready.

Oh, he would have married her by Christmas. Asked her, at least. But something held him back, pulled against his touching her, made his shoulders tense and his eyes refuse hers. Through all those years of sitting on her front porch, of picture shows and window shopping, of fountain lemonades and winter walks, he could have asked her—and yet he didn't, until he found himself a dancing man, a waiter, and no fit husband. Now at fifty-two he was unemployed altogether, jobless on account of Papa Tutoni's heart attack.

Business Closed through the Summer, the sign on the front door read.

"Collect unemployment," Papa's son, the sauce cook, had said. "We all need a rest," he'd said. He'd had tears in his eyes and his hands were white and smooth beneath the cuffs of his good suit. He was on his way to the hospital to see his father and didn't want to argue with a dancing waiter.

"I'll call you when Papa gets well," he said without much enthusiasm.

So Hazard left the Flanagans' telephone number in the kitchen and packed his bag. He didn't want to stay above the vacant restaurant all summer. He needed people around him. He needed family.

That's what he was thinking as he stared at the ceiling of his room. How he needed someone and how more than likely at six o'clock he would hear Pansy's voice below in the kitchen, pick her soft laughter out of Jane's rollicking loud humor, and know that she, pretending no surprise at finding him there, would offer him only a fleeting smile across the supper table. She wouldn't expect or demand anything.

There was a humming in the wall. Hazard raised up on the bed, cocked his head as if one ear heard better than the other, and stared out into space as though he expected to eventually see the sound. The humming stopped, paused it seemed for a shallow tremulous breath, and then started up again.

It was the girl Casey in her daddy's old room. Hazard had forgotten all about her. What was she doing here, anyway? He couldn't remember having seen her since she was a tiny thing and her mother, looking so young and bright-eyed, had brought her to spend an earlier summer while David was in the Pacific.

Surely they came more often than he knew, probably at Christmas, for Hazard made a point of avoiding the Flanagans' at Christmas. He always told them he couldn't get off from work, but the truth was that he felt uncomfortable with them on holidays. He didn't want to be included in the Flanagans' holiday because they felt sorry for him, so he always arrived after the first of the year, bringing gifts bought at the pre-inventory sales, to put under the tree Jane left up through Epiphany.

So their pasts had never touched, and he didn't know this Casey who'd sat next to him in the kitchen nibbling at her lunch while he and Jane had bantered, saying nothing but providing comfort to him in that moment of transition he always felt between standing on the back porch and being in his room upstairs.

Now it seemed to him the humming was somehow tearful, pushed out by sighs.

"Who's there?" he called, rapping lightly on the wall above his head.

The humming stopped.

"I say, who's there?"

Silence. He rapped again, determined to make contact with the voice that seemed so melancholy to him.

"It's me—Casey," a voice said finally. "I didn't mean to bother you." Her voice seemed close, as if she had pressed her lean cool cheek against the wall by his head.

Hazard lifted his hand to the wall again, a long bony hand with even, clean nails and a sprinkling of fine gray hairs. His hand surprised him, for it suddenly looked old, an undeniable evidence that he was truly fifty-two. What have I done? he thought suddenly. What can I account for since I was her age?

Instead of knocking again, he slipped off the bed and went down the hall to the door of David's room. The girl was standing at the head of the bed close to the wall as if she were still listening for him. Her suitcase was open on the narrow bed, and some of her clothes had been unpacked and were separated into piles on the spread. He knocked once gently and pushed it open.

"Oh," Casey said, turning her attention from the wall. "I'm sorry. I just start singing sometimes." She looked down at the underclothes on the bed, then lifted them quickly back into the suitcase and closed the lid. She wanted to be alone. Couldn't he see that?

"I don't want to bother you," Hazard said, easing in. The room looked like it always had. The rug on which David had long ago spilled chemicals from his laboratory set was still there, blotches of faded color around his desk. It looked vaguely like a boy's room, and yet more bland then he'd remembered, as if it were ageless, sexless, void of any personality. Casey looked ageless and sexless, too.

"Your daddy's room," Hazard said, nodding at the plaid curtains as if they especially reminded him of David. Actually he was remembering his first glimpse of the boy when he must have been eight years old, dark David of the shadowy eyes, the veiled face, the silent kitchen helper, solitary roamer. He had been at the table next to Pansy that first night. David was as much a part of Hazard's life as anyone. Now it looked like Casey would be, too. "Yeah, David's room," he said again.

"Uh-huh." Casey looked at the room, too. She seemed to be searching for proof that it really was her father's room. She sighed with defeat.

"I used to come in here sometimes when your daddy was a boy. We'd talk sometimes. He was quiet, though.

Always busy doing something and looked like he didn't want to be interrupted. You favor him, you know. Got those eyes and that mouth. Gimme a smile. Yeah, there it is. Just like David."

Casey sat down on the edge of the bed, and Hazard took it as an invitation to himself to settle in the only chair in the room. He turned the desk chair around so he faced the girl. "What were you humming?" he asked.

Casey looked down at her suitcase and then at her hands, which she rubbed together as if to warm them. "It Had to Be You," she whispered.

"That's it! That's right!" Hazard grinned and slapped his knees. "I knew I knew it, but I just couldn't bring it to mind. *It had to be you*," he sang, slightly off key. "*It had to be you ... I wandered around and fin-al-ly found ... Some-body who ... Could make me feel true ... Could make me feel blue—*" He hesitated, running his tongue against his upper lip while he thought.

"*And even be glad, just to be sad—*" Casey sang softly, the beginning of a smile on her lips.

"*—Thinking of you.*" Hazard joined in with a snap of his fingers to show he'd remembered. He was on his feet, poised for action.

"Sing, sing," he urged. "You know it. Sing!"

"*Some others I've seen—*" Casey began louder than before. She was watching him move. The old rug was like glass under him as he spun and the afternoon light from the window spotted him gently. A hand here. A shoulder. Full light in his face. "*Might never be mean ... Might never be cross or try to be boss ... But they wouldn't do—*" Her voice rose to a torchy pitch while Hazard twirled. "*For no-bo-dy else gave me a thrill ...*

*With all your faults I love you still . . . It had to be you,
won-der-ful you, had to be you—"*

"Hot damn, you're good," Hazard said, collapsing in
his chair. "Why, you got the voice of an angel. You
gonna be a singer, I know it! I'm in show business
myself, and talent don't have to knock me in the head
before I see it!"

"That's what Mama's doing," Casey said. She had
looked back to her hands; the spell they had created
between themselves was broken.

"What's that?" Hazard leaned forward to hear her.

"Singing. She's singing in a club in Columbia. She
works in the bank like she always did, but she's singing at night. This man heard her singing at a party she
went to with some of Daddy's friends and he told her
she could sing at his restaurant if she wanted to. She
went down there the next day. It was a nightclub and
that scared her a little, but the man was real nice and
she says it's a nice place."

Casey paused to get her breath. Hazard thought it
might be the most she'd ever uttered at one time.

"Daddy's in Korea," she went on. "That makes Mama
nervous and she didn't like being home every night
thinking about how Daddy might get hurt. She said she
needed to keep busy. So she took this singing job and
I came here to spend the summer so I wouldn't be by
myself all the time. I didn't mind being by myself a bit,
but Mama said she didn't want to have me to worry
about too, so she wrote to Grandma about it and
Grandma called up long-distance on the telephone and
said I should come." She looked up, straight into
Hazard's eyes. "Mama bought some dresses to wear

when she sings. A red one and a black one and one with blue sparkles on it because it would look pretty under the lights. I don't like dresses. I wear pants, even to school. When the teacher complained, Mama went after class and showed her where there's nothing in the dress code except about being neat and clean and wearing shoes." She smiled, believing that if any need had arisen to do so, she had successfully redeemed her mother.

"Sounds real fine," Hazard agreed. "All summer here, huh?" He slapped his knees. "Me, too, I reckon. Haven't told Jane yet, so don't go blabbing to her. I work in a restaurant, too, you see, and the owner got sick and closed up until he's better. I didn't see much point in hanging around there, so here I am, ready to pickle, shuck corn, string beans. Whatever comes along."

Casey just looked at him.

"Well, I'm thinking how Miss Pansy just might be coming for supper tonight," he continued. He was feeling better. Having explained himself aloud, his situation didn't sound so bad. "You're acquainted with Miss Pansy, I reckon."

"I reckon I am." Casey couldn't help smiling at him.

"What you grinning about?" He looked pained and then turned on his grin. "You've heard about me! I know it! I can tell!"

"Just from Grandma and Pansy. Sometimes, like at Christmas, Pansy will get a worried look and say to Grandma, 'Wonder where that man is this cold winter evening?' and Grandma will say right back, 'Off somewhere, causing a hazard.' Then they laugh until Mama comes to see what's the matter and then they get quiet, like you're a secret between them. Grandma and Pansy get right silly together sometimes."

"There you go!" Hazard laughed. "Two little bantam hens!"

"That's not all," Casey said, beginning to enjoy herself. "Pansy said you were a millstone around her neck."

"Said what?" Hazard had the feeling he was hearing more than he wanted to.

"She said Hades could freeze over before she married you. She said she doesn't want to get married to anybody, but she's tired of waiting to turn you down."

"When'd she say that?"

"Just this afternoon. After you came upstairs, Grandma and I walked down to her house. Grandma said we were going because Pansy was so anxious to see me, but all the talk was about you."

"It was, huh?" Hazard rubbed his chin as if he were seriously contemplating this information.

"You and Uncle Taylor," Casey added. "And Taylor's new girl friend." Casey got up and went to the window. She ran her fingers along the edge of the plaid curtain while she looked out. "Grandma doesn't know what to do with Taylor, you know. Pansy says he's twenty-eight years old and what can anybody do with him? But Grandma says Pansy doesn't know what it's like having a grown son showing no more sense than Taylor does. He's always off racing that car of his, you know. Grandma says if Taylor would just settle down with some nice girl, she and Grandma would let him run the lumberyard all by himself. They'd turn these three rooms up here into a little apartment for them and not charge a bit of rent. They'd take a trip to Florida."

"My room!" Hazard said before he could stop himself.

"A sitting room, a bedroom, and I think a nursery," Casey said, "because Grandpa says that's the only circumstance that will get Taylor married. Grandma says 'God forbid' to that."

"My room!" Hazard boomed.

"Grandma says Taylor brings girls through her house like it was an inspection post, because he knows these racetrack girls aren't going to get any encouragement from her. Well, I'm supposed to be setting the table. You coming?"

"I've got to wash up," Hazard said.

He sat in the room after Casey had gone and watched dust mots stirred by her movement in the stream of light across the desk. All this talk about marriage worried him. It was like they had all latched on to the subject of his personal affections like fruit-flies on a spoiling peach. Even Casey seemed to be in on it. Well, he'd wanted to be prodded a little—he could admit that, at least to himself. But he didn't want to be peeled, pitted, and preserved. Not yet, anyway.

"Oh well," he sighed like a man who had already given up. He leaned back in the chair, his hands supporting his thin neck, and stared up at the ceiling. He was still sitting there when Jane called him to supper.

· 4 ·

*J*ane Flanagan *turned* the turnip salad out of its steaming pot liquor and into a colander in the sink.

"Good Lord, it's hot in here," she said over her shoulder to Pansy, who had just come in the back door and was arranging curls around her face with a deft finger. "You'll just melt if you linger a minute. Go on in the parlor. Taylor's in there. Ben, too, I think. And Casey's around here somewhere."

They looked at each other, silently acknowledging the presence of Hazard in the house.

"I'll stay in here and help you," Pansy said, although she made no move toward the bubbling stove.

"Well, you can touch up the flowers on the table if you want to do something," Jane said. "It's been so dry lately, I don't have anything but some azalea sprigs."

Pansy stepped into the dining room. The air was close, faintly tinged with kitchen heat and smells from the stove. The shades were pulled, but a light evening breeze edged around them and sucked at their centers.

She went to the window and raised the shades. Light broke in soft patterns on the rosy wallpaper and the faded green rug. Jane's dining room was Pansy's favorite part of the house. She loved the heavy dark mahogany sideboard and breakfront that gleamed with old silver and delicately flowered crackled china. The table had been set and the chairs pushed into place.

Six places. Jane and Ben at the ends. Casey next to Ben. Taylor next to her. On the other side of the table, her own place at Ben's left. Hazard beside her, but with a space between. An empty space. She felt a sudden urge to fill that void and so she stepped into it, one hand on her own chair, one on Hazard's. The wood was warm, the fabric slick and worn with pulled damask threads from years of being sat upon. The cloth was warm, too, as if a body had just been there. Hazard, who slouched in his seat. Who always looked careless at the table, as if he wanted to prepare them for any mishap that might occur. Of course, his attitude was conducive to accidents—his was the water goblet that tumbled, his roll crumbled around his plate. His coffee cup sloshed onto the table cloth. And so he was apologetic and contrite and aggravating.

"Oh," she moaned, imagining him there, and pressed her palms to her face, fingertips against her eyebrows. Her forehead felt hot, flushed with thinking about Hazard, and with knowing he was somewhere in the house, maybe in the room above her.

She knew what that room looked like, for she'd passed it many times on her way to inspect new curtains, help fit a dress, visit a sick child. She knew how the washstand tilted a little on the uneven floor and how a block of wood was slipped under the back leg to steady it. She knew what the bed looked like, a double bed with a blue chenille spread washed to hard flat knots of cotton. She even knew the view from the window, how the Baptist Church spire showed above the trees to the left and how if one stood in just the proper spot, the beginning of her own walk was visible, a glimmer of a white post, a marigold or two.

She knew the room but she couldn't imagine Hazard in it, didn't want to think about his shabby clothes in the open wardrobe or his shaving kit on the washstand or the bed stripped of its chenille and laid white and crisp with sheets as slick as the tablecloth she was now touching. She dropped her hands to her sides. Oh, Hazard, she thought. What will become of us?

There was laughter from the parlor. It was Hazard. He was greeting Taylor and Ben with hugs. Slapping his thighs. Making a joke for Casey. All this while he waited for her.

As surely as she knew he was there, Pansy knew he stood expectantly, his feet shifting, his legs as weak as hers. And now his stomach curled, his hands sweated slightly, his grinning face contorted with hope played against dismay that she had finally failed him and was not there.

She backed away from the table and started toward the kitchen door.

I must see if Jane needs me, she was thinking. Jane is always left with all the responsibility while I flit around, thinking foolishness.

She paused again, hesitating between the two doors, when abruptly and silently, the door from the living room opened and there he was, wearing that cheap blue plaid jacket she'd wanted to discard for years, and that grin, that idiotic, no-better-than-Dwayne-Pickens expression that betrayed his childishness, his expectancy, his fright.

"Hazard," she said because the rest of the family was

gathering behind him, waiting to get to the table. But he just stood there, thinking that he was reading something new in her expression, something that sparkled on her face and made her look younger, even twenty-five years younger, like she had that first night he'd seen her when he'd felt with such shattering alacrity what he'd been all this time recovering from—here was the woman he'd always care about. This was the person he'd never want to lose.

"Old Mr. Tutoni had a heart attack and he's in the hospital and they've closed the restaurant till he gets better or else he dies. Either way, I don't see much future in it," he began.

He had never been so awkward in his life. Never had his hands seemed so big and useless. Never had his head ballooned and lightened as if he were full of air or smoke. He felt himself evaporating under her gaze. His mouth formed heavy, careful, unspoken words around his tongue. I've always been a salesman, he thought. A salesman, a con artist, a dancing man. His feet moved under him, starting a slow brush step.

Oh, no, good heavens, he's going to dance, Pansy thought with horror. And she raised her hand to stop him.

Hazard did stop, but it wasn't Pansy's hand midair that halted him but the true and crucial knowledge that she would that very minute protect him against himself, would put out those careful fingers, so reserved in touching, to catch him as if she truly believed she could.

"I want to marry you, Pansy," he said before he could stop himself. Then, knowing full well what he was risking, he abandoned himself to it: "I've wanted to marry you for twenty-five years and I figure it's time I give you a chance to refuse me, if that's what you're aiming to do."

If he had shot straight at her soul, he could not have pierced her more completely.

"Why, Hazard," she said as if he'd just invited her to the picture show, "Of course I'll marry you."

Jane was behind her, a platter of fried chicken held like an offering on her arms. "What's this?" she asked, setting the plate at Ben's end of the table. "You all come on to the table. Supper's ready. Casey, come help me, honey. I've just got to get the biscuits up."

They stumbled into their places like drunks, their faces blustery and wide with the spectacle they'd just witnessed while Jane slipped bowls between their shoulders to the table.

"Pour out the water, Pansy," she said.

In all those years Pansy had never failed to bring the pitcher from the sideboard to pour full each goblet. Now she rose and put her hands on the pitcher, felt the cool weight of it. It was such a precious thing, this wedding pitcher of Jane's. She had never noticed before how slender the handle was or what strength it assumed against the water. It pulled at her wrist and she put up her other hand to steady it.

"Hazard has asked me to marry him," she said to Jane, although she faced the sideboard and the pitcher, her back to the table where Hazard sat struck-dumb but with tears rimming his eyes. "He has asked me and I have accepted."

"Well, hallelujah!" Jane said, as if the decision had been made only seconds before her patience gave out. "Now let's eat."

• 5 •

Nobody slept well. Casey awoke with the early light to the damp, warm heat of her father's rumpled bed. She had dreamed about him.

He stood on the front stoop of their military duplex in his flight suit with a duffel bag over his shoulder. Her mother was in the doorway behind him, her hands on the screen, as if she were about to come out. Her father looked across the yard at a little girl who was running toward him. The girl didn't look like Casey—she was much too young and had blond curls—but Casey knew the girl was she and that her father was calling her to hurry up and hug him.

But just as he put out his arms to her, the military police appeared, one on either side of him, and her father dropped his arms abruptly and stood at attention, eyes blank, face set like a uniform-clad mannequin she'd seen in an "Uncle Sam Wants You" exhibit.

The little girl pulled at her father's pants leg and tried to squirm into his arms, but the M.P.s shoved her away. She attacked his duffel bag in a frenzy, but the bag was heavy and banged against her chest, knocking her off the stoop onto the ground. Still her father didn't acknowledge her but marched stiffly to the jeep be-

tween the M.P.s. The child sat on the ground screaming as he got into the jeep and it pulled away. Finally
she got up and turned to the house, where her mother
was still standing, her hands pushed through the
screen. There were two ragged holes where her hands
had gone through.

Casey lay on her back, trying to remember every fine
detail of the dream, as if by recalling it perfectly she
could gain some defense against it. She shut her eyes
and then squeezed them tight in concentration. What
had her mother been wearing? Her clothing had
seemed to shimmer against the screen. One of those
singing dresses, that's what it must have been. One
of those silly sequined scraps of cloth she'd paid a
small fortune for. Casey hated those dresses. She
opened her eyes to make the image of them go away
and then lay still, gnawing her lip. She knew the dream
wasn't really about her mother anyway. It had been
about her father. It had been about going to war as if
he didn't really mind, like it was easy for him because
he was doing his job and he didn't have to think about
it. Like nothing mattered to him as much as flying did,
even if it meant flying in a war. Why did he want to
fly anyway?

It was a question she could never ask him, fearful
perhaps that he wouldn't want to tell her, or, even
worse, that he would admit he didn't know the answer.
She didn't want his life to be a mystery to him, not like
hers so often was to her. Grown-ups never seemed to
have very good answers to the questions that bothered
her, so she'd learned to look out for herself, imagining
answers at least as satisfactory as the ones she futilely
gleaned from other people.

So she lay there imagining her father alone above the world, looking down on trees that were thick splotches of green and rivers that were tiny stationary streams and cities like Christmas-tree villages. He couldn't see any people, she was sure of that. No children looking up to discover fanciful pictures in the clouds. No parents fearfully studied the sky. No worries of earthly things followed him there; she could imagine him exhilarated, complete, content. Those were good reasons for doing something, even if you couldn't say them out loud.

Down the hall in the bathroom, water was running. Casey got up, straightened her disheveled pajamas, and padded into Taylor's room. Empty, but alive with color. Pictures of cars, gleaming Fords, grinning Chevvies, Plymouths, Hudsons. A glossy of Taylor's stripped Mercury that he kept locked in the lumberyard between races was hung above his bed.

Taylor might spend his days in the lumberyard, but his mind was forever on racing. Cars were the only things he took seriously and the only subject about which he was reticent. Only from hearing him talk to her father did Casey know how he loved speed.

"Morning," Taylor said from behind her. He was wearing a towel and his hair was a mass of tangled rusty curls. Casey liked the way he let his hair grow instead of shearing it close on his neck and around his ears like her father did. She liked Taylor's not having so many rules to follow and his wearing sloppy clothes and scuffed saddle oxfords.

"Forgot there was a lady on the hall," he said, going past her to his closet. "Excuse me a minute." He ducked behind the door and came out wearing his pants.

"I've got something to tell you, Taylor," Casey said. "Actually it's something to ask you. It's about Dwayne Pickens." She sat down on the bed while Taylor slipped into his shirt.

"No need to worry, sugar," Taylor said. "He's harmless. Dwayne and I go way back. He was your daddy's friend, you know, back before anybody knew he was retarded. It happened so fast, like somebody opened up his ears one night and all his brains spilled out. Just that quick, it seemed like. Of course, I was just a kid and I thought everybody was smarter than me. It came as a surprise, I can tell you."

"Grandma told me," Casey said. "This is something else. It's about me and Dwayne. You see, I met him yesterday and he thinks I'm a boy. Grandmother says he doesn't like girls very much."

Taylor stopped fiddling with his tie and looked at her through the mirror. The child he saw surprised him. He had never given Casey much thought. She was, after all, just a little kid who came twice a year with parents who hovered over her with good behavior and nutrition on their minds. She had always been outside his reach, always so delicate and quiet, even foreign to him, although he had to admit she had her daddy's looks. Still he couldn't remember ever holding her or even really talking to her. He had never felt like an uncle.

Yet here she was, his niece. How old? Twelve probably, and beginning to grow up. In two or three years she'd be going out with boys, then off to college, then married maybe. He didn't know. He didn't know her well enough to know if she wanted those things, if her dreams had frills and music in them. All he knew was that she understood something about Dwayne Pickens, she felt something for that bumbling crazy man in his dirty baseball cap. She was asking him to help her protect it.

"I won't tell him," Taylor said, turning to look at her straight-on.

"I didn't really lie to him," Casey said. She stood up and ran her finger across the photographed fender of a 1949 Ford.

"You don't have to explain, Casey." Taylor waved his hand at the pictures. "We've all got things we don't want to explain."

"Thanks, Taylor."

"Now let's get some breakfast. I've got three hours at the lumberyard and then a race at two o'clock."

"Can I come?" Casey wanted to know.

"Let's put it this way. If you're there, I'll give you a ride home. Just don't tell your grandmother. The best plan is to get money for the pictures. Thirty-five cents gets you in the gate and a bottle of pop." He dipped into his pocket. "Here's fifteen cents more for peanuts. What the hell, it's like being at a circus anyway."

HAZARD COULD hear them talking. He socked his pillow behind his head and looked at the ceiling. He couldn't help thinking that his restless, tumbling night was an omen of discomfort to come. Already he had a headache, and his stomach burned with indigestion—or was it hunger? He couldn't remember eating a thing last night. All he could remember was Pansy.

He hadn't talked to her, not the kind of talk he'd expected to have. People in their situation were supposed to make plans, to be heady with the future. But walking her home, the still warm night close against them, he couldn't tell her he didn't have a plan, had no intentions for the future except to marry her.

He had looked up, hoping for stars, but the clouds were as thick and low as fog. Pansy was worrying about the possibility of a polio epidemic, but he only half listened to her because he was thinking about himself and about her, too, but not about her life. Her job, her house, her daily existence, seemed too concrete, too indestructible. He wanted to think about stars or nothing at all.

"They've had seven cases of poliomyelitis in the next county already, and it's just the middle of June," Pansy was saying.

He put his hand on her arm, hoping his touch would stop her, but she went on. "Dr. Kemble says this might be the summer for us. You know how we've been spared. All these years and only a few scattered cases, most of them quite mild. But this might be our year for an epidemic." She had taken on her doctor's receptionist tone and her arm stiffened under his grasp. "I suppose I should have talked to Jane about it, but I didn't see how she could help but get Casey down here. There's polio in South Carolina, too, you know. Once hot weather comes, no place is safe. Still I wouldn't want the responsibility of a child this time of year."

"Well, here we are," Hazard said halfheartedly at Pansy's steps. "I reckon we should talk some, Pansy."

"Yes we should," she said with a sigh and moved to the porch swing while Hazard stayed on the step. Pansy seemed as unapproachable as the subject did.

The swing rocked gently, and Hazard watched the slight restless movement of her pale dress in the window light.

"I was born here, you know," Pansy said from the rocking swing. "My daddy was the only doctor in town for a long time and we could have afforded a finer house than this, but after Mama died, Daddy didn't want to move. He thought it would be like leaving her here if we moved someplace else. I was glad he didn't want to go. I like this house and there's always been Jane right down the street. We had good domestic help then, and I did for Daddy the best I could. Thank goodness, he thought women should have occupations. He taught me to keep his records and do the books besides being his receptionist. When he died and Dr. Kemble came, I knew as much about Daddy's practice as anybody. All the figures in the ledger were mine. Dr. Kemble can't manage without me anymore than Daddy could have."

"I'll need to look for a job," Hazard said. "I was thinking I might ask Ben if there's anything down at the lumberyard, just to get me started on something."

"We can talk about that tomorrow," Pansy said. She sighed again. "Come sit by me, Hazard."

Right then, at that moment when she was asking him to come to her, he wished he were younger. The wish overpowered him, even frightened him with its surge of regret. He wished her father would come out that very minute. They would shake hands like they used to fifteen years ago and then Hazard would stand, his arm firmly about Pansy's shoulder, and say, "Your daughter has agreed to be my wife and I hope we have your blessing."

Is that what he would have said? Was that how it would have been so many years ago, if he had only understood that time didn't stand still, that he would someday be jobless, penniless. Fifty-two.

"What is it, Hazard?"

"I was thinking about your daddy. I was thinking about the past."

"There's no point in it," Pansy said lightly. "It's over and done with. Besides, I feel so happy tonight, so new. I don't want to think about regrets if we have any. I want to think about the future. Why, we have a wedding to see to. Even the most simple wedding requires careful planning. And then there's the wedding trip to think about."

Hazard could see her mind clicking through the details. There was nothing for him to do. He had played his part already, acted it out like a fool in front of the whole family. Now the rest seemed safely in Pansy's capable hands.

"Aren't you going to sit, Hazard?" she was asking him.

"Not tonight," he said. "I think I'll get on home. Like you said, we can talk about it tomorrow."

He waited for her to get out of the swing and come to him. The light through the glass front of her door edged her curls, put a shiny orb on her nose. He bent forward and pressed his mouth against her cheek, touching the light with his lips. Her face was warm. Her hands moved smoothly to his shoulders and he felt fingers through his damp jacket. Their faces moved spontaneously forward, but he knew she was hesitating, wanting to say something to him. He paused while his hands pressed into the curls along her neck.

"If you don't want to do this, Hazard," she said, "you must tell me now."

He couldn't answer her. For the life of him, no words came into his head that could say how scared he was, how happy, how completely undone. He pressed his mouth against hers and felt a little sigh as she accepted his answer, his confusion, his feeble entreaty that she was everything to him.

"Well, good night," she said.

"Good night," he muttered, kissing her lightly again. Suddenly he wanted very much to stay with her. He felt a swift, desperate panic that told him that by leaving her he would be losing something precious, some irretrievable moment in which to seal forever his intentions toward her, but nevertheless he stumbled off the porch and made his way down the walk to the Flanagans' without looking back.

If he had turned back, he would have seen Pansy turning the key in her front door (Why, he'd forgotten to unlock it for her!) and drop the key and her bag on the hall table. Then the house was suddenly dark, for Pansy clicked off the hall light and went through the shadows down the hall to her room.

There was no moon, just a hazy blackness outside her window, so she let up the shade and undressed by the distant window light from the house next door. Her bed was warm and her light summer gown clung to her skin, although she didn't feel the close heat of her house, only the sensation of being alive and healthy. She pulled the sheet up as if she anticipated a shiver, for she did. She expected every physical sensation she could imagine. She lay there waiting, remembering every word Hazard had said, every touch. She

clasped her hands together across the sheet and remembered his kiss. She waited for every moment to
relive itself, and while she waited, lying still in her
bed with the thick buzzing air of summer around her,
she went to sleep.

⟫ 6 ⟪

The noon whistle from the lumberyard had sounded and dinner had been served in the Flanagan kitchen before Casey saw Dwayne Pickens again. She was alone in the kitchen, having taken over the dishes from her weary grandmother, when she heard a clumping sound on the back porch and turned to find him peering in through the screen at her.

"Come on in, Dwayne," she said, although she hurried to wipe her hands and move away from the dishpan. What would he think of a boy doing the dishes?

Dwayne didn't budge.

"You can come in," Casey called again. She quickly spread a tea towel over the drying dishes and pulled the stopper out of the sink. The sudsy water gurgled away.

"I can't come in nobody's house," Dwayne said. He ducked his head and Casey saw only the oily stained crown of his baseball cap and the hands he twisted nervously in front of him.

"Why not?" she asked, pushing open the door. "I invited you."

"You did?"

"Sure I did. I said, 'Come on in, Dwayne.' "

He was grinning at her. "That's right, you did." He frowned and ducked his head again. "Mama says I don't go in people's houses."

"Then I'll come out."

They sat down on the steps.

"Hey boy, whatcha been doing all day?" he wanted to know.

"Nothing."

"I been cutting grass," Dwayne said, happy to have something to report. "Every Saturday I got to cut the grass at Alva's. Then come up here and cut the grass at Mama's. Mama's got a little yard, but Alva! You know my brother Alva? He's got that yard where we used to live, big as a ballpark near about. I fill up that gas tank and I pull that cord and there I go a-mowing and a-mowing. I hate that yard now Alva's got bushes in it and little flowers don't look like nothing but if'n I hit one, watch out! I get paid, though. Three dollars for Alva's. One dollar for Mama's. That's four dollars a week in the summertime to buy things with." He pulled his money out of his jeans and counted it on his knee. "One-two-three-four." He grinned. "See. Four dollars."

"What do you plan to buy with it?" Casey wanted to know.

"I don't know." He scratched under his cap. "Sometimes I buy some baseball cards or some comic books. One time I bought everybody in Hollis Drugstore a soda. It costed two seventy-five! Sometimes I just save it and get something big. I have to buy a lot of baseballs. Them and chewing 'bacca."

"I know where you could spend it today," Casey said. "We could go to the races at the fairgrounds. Do you ever do that?"

"Taylor goes there," Dwayne said. "I see him there in his car. He races—*va-ro-o-m* he goes around the track." He dropped the money and put his hands on an imaginary wheel. The wheel spun in his hands and he fought frantically for control. "He's spinning," Dwayne yelled in his announcer's voice. "He can't come out of the curve. That Ford's on top of him. They're gonna crash!" Dwayne made a skidding sound. "Pow! Bang! *Ba-a-m-a-lam!* And the cars are out of the race! What about the drivers? Here they come! They're all right! They're O.K.!"

Dwayne applauded madly. So did Casey.

"If we start now, we can walk out there by two o'clock, can't we?"

"You got to tell your grandma. You always got to tell somebody when you go off," Dwayne said, collecting his money from the ground.

"I will. I'll be back in a minute." Casey tiptoed through the dining room into the parlor where Jane lay with a cold cloth on her forehead.

"Grandma," she whispered from across the room. "I'm going out. I'll be back by supper."

No answer.

"Grandma?" Casey hesitated and then slipped back into the kitchen. "Well," she said to Dwayne, stuffing her own money into her pants pocket, "I told her."

IT WAS after two when they reached the fairgrounds on the other side of town, but walking along with Dwayne, Casey didn't really care what time they got there. She was too busy listening to him tell her about the stores they were passing and then the houses. It seemed that he knew everyone in town and had some opinion about each of them he didn't mind sharing.

They walked slowly, the afternoon sun boiling on their backs. Dwayne tossed a baseball in front of him, catching it effortlessly, as if it were as familiar an action as walking, and just as necessary.

"Folks named Post live there," he said, rolling his head in the direction of a big brick house with white columns and a carefully manicured lawn. "She don't like me. No-siree! One time my brother Alva, he wanted me to do yard work. He come up to our house and he says to Mama, he says—" Dwayne stopped and ducked his head to think. He wanted to get Alva's words exactly right. "He says, 'Mama, that boy's got to do something 'sides play ball. He's got to learn some responsibil-ity. He's got to cut grass.'" Dwayne laughed out loud, proud of successfully mocking Alva. "So Alva gives me this paper with all these people on it and he says, 'You take your mower down there and cut grass.' So I did. I came right here." He stopped again in front of the beautifully landscaped lawn.

"There was people all out there—in the back, too. Everywhere you'd want to look. They were walking around eating and talking and listening to music. But I went right on and cut that grass. I said, 'Excuse me,' but Lordy, it was hard going 'tween all them folks. They kept moving, you see, and they had those little tables with them little legs and lots of little chairs. Anyhow, that Mrs. Post, she come running out there and she says mean things to me. Ugly, ugly things, like you wouldn't hear me saying to nobody. And I says

Alva gave me this paper and it says I'm coming here to cut this grass. And she says you get outa my yard and don't you come back. Boy, was Alva mad at me. He was as mad as that woman was." Dwayne sighed and tossed the ball high. He ran forward a little to catch it in his bare palm. "I don't like cutting grass no way. I don't want a job. People yelling at you and all. You got a job?"

"Nope. I go to school in the winter and in the summer I just mess around. Who lives there?" Casey pointed at a yellow house with aqua trim.

"Oh, that's Monty's house. Ain't it the prettiest little thing! Monty's the man at the picture show. He takes the money and then he gives you half a ticket in case you want to keep it. He don't take money from me, though. I just go right on in. Monty says, 'Hey boy, where you going?' and I say, 'In here to see this picture show and it better be a goodun!' You be nice to folks and they be nice to you right back. That's one thing for sure."

"I think it's neat, your knowing everybody like you do," Casey said.

"Yeah." Dwayne puffed himself up a little and grinned at her. "I never lived no other place. Never been nowhere, neither, excepting that time they took me off to that school. Alva said it was a school, but I didn't see no school to it. First I went to the school right here, you see." Dwayne's smile had faded as he remembered. "I went a long time, but I got so tired of it. All them little kids. Every year, more little kids. Couldn't none of them play ball worth a hoot. So I quit going. Mama and Daddy and me was all right. It was Alva wanted me to go off to that place and learn something. So I went. Only there weren't no school to it. It was more like a hospital. They wouldn't let me listen to the radio there. That's what I didn't like the most. They says to me, 'Dwayne, them ballgames just get you all worked up,' and they took my radio away. Mama said they wanted me to rest up, but that weren't it. They didn't want no noise in that place. They didn't want nobody having a good time listening to the ballgames. That's all it was."

They walked on in silence. After a while, Dwayne tossed the ball again and ran forward to get it. "I ain't never going to that place again," he said. "Not ever."

THE RACETRACK was a ragged oval of dirt hewed into the middle of a pasture that lay inside the fairground fence.

"Long time back, they raced horses out here," Dwayne said. "When the fair comes, this is where you get to see fireworks, great big ones popping all over the sky." He pulled out his money and gave the man at the gate a bill.

"Hey boy," the man said. "What you doing out here at the races? You ain't planning to drive no cars, is you?"

"Don't have no car. I got me a bicycle, anyhow," Dwayne retorted, his hand stuck out for his change.

"We've come to see Taylor Flanagan," Casey said, dropping her money into the man's hand. "He's my uncle. Do you know where he is?"

"Over there in the infield, most likely. But don't you go over there. It's dangerous, ain't it, boy? Ain't it, Dwayne? You two just get a seat right there in the stands and you'll be seeing Taylor by and by. He'll come flying around here, big as anything in that Mercury of his. You seen that car run, boy?"

"Sure I seen it," Dwayne said impatiently, tired of having to prove himself. "I seen it lots of times."

Casey pulled him along, anxious to get a good seat before the race started. The stands consisted of three rows of weathered bleachers separated from the track by a chicken-wire fence.

"Let's go to the top," she said to Dwayne, wanting to get as high up and away from the other spectators as possible, where she could see everything.

The stands were filling up. They squirmed over pocketbooks and children to get to the far end of the third row. Once settled, Casey saw that most of the fans had driven their cars into the field surrounding the track and were perched on their hoods, awaiting the action. Some were leaning back against their windshields, their faces to the sun, mouths gaping while they napped. Others sat up straight, balancing on fenders while they drank beer and ate sandwiches out of waxed paper. A girl in shorts and halter lay on her stomach on top of a car with her bare feet hanging off the back, getting a tan. She flipped her head from side to side restlessly, as if she were suffering, and eventually she propped up on one elbow and called to the young man in a cowboy hat who was wandering around the other cars to bring her a soda.

"Anything cold!" she said. "You hear me, Frankie, something *cold!*" She sat up on the car, her legs crossed under her, her back arched, shoulders back, blond ponytail catching the sunlight.

"That's Taylor's new girl friend," Dwayne said, bobbing his head in the girl's direction.

Casey was still watching her. So this was a racetrack girl. She was one of those girls Taylor brought through her grandmother's house like it was an inspection post. Well, she didn't see any reason why Grandma wouldn't approve of this one. She sure was pretty enough.

Frankie had returned with the bottle of soda, which the girl took from him. She lifted his cowboy hat off, twirled it mischieviously around on her hand, and plopped it down askew on his head.

"Don't Taylor need you?" she asked him. "Some mechanic you are!"

"Naw, car's running good, Gwen. He's all set."

"I sure do hope so. It's just too hot out here. I wish they'd get started." Gwen pushed her ponytail up on top of her head and let it fall again. "You tell Taylor I'll be right here after the race," she said. "I'll be steaming, too."

"I ain't tellin' him that." Frankie laughed. He patted the hood of the car. "You want him to keep his mind on what he's doing out there, don't you?"

"I guess so," Gwen said. She lifted the bottle to her lips, swung back her head, and took a big swallow. Casey thought she looked like a calendar model. Like she'd been studying poses and was proceeding to practice them one at a time.

"Well, I got to get going," Frankie said.

"Thanks for the cold drink," Gwen said sweetly. "Now you tell Taylor I'm waiting."

The girl flopped back down on the car, so Casey

turned her attention to the track itself. She could see Taylor in the infield beside his Mercury. The car had been stripped of its chrome and was painted a gaudy bright green. A big number three was stenciled on its door.

While she watched him, thinking how distant he was and yet surprised at how visible this secret life of his was proving to be, Taylor crawled through the window of the car and disappeared as if into a tunnel, gloved hands sinking last into the black interior of the gutted car. The automobile shuddered and sprang forward, followed by other cars that pulled out onto the track in some prearranged order. Their engines were like discordant music, each instrument trying to outsound the others as their drivers listened intently to their pitch and rhythm, the hidden strain of victory or defeat their cars predicted.

The crowd stood up in unison, as if the roar of the cars commanded them. Then the loudspeaker crackled over the idling engines and a parched rattling rendition of "The Star Spangled Banner" blared over them as Dwayne whipped off his baseball cap and Gwen, still atop the car, pretended to sleep so she wouldn't have to stand up.

The music warbled to a defeated halt, and Casey watched the flag fall in front of the cars. They lurched across the starting line, nose to tail, like rabbit dogs hunting a common scent.

"They're off!" the announcer shouted into the sputtering microphone.

Dwayne and Casey were still on their feet, giving the green Mercury their protective attention. Casey watched the cars moving into the first turn and felt her legs buckle. It was the same feeling she had when she saw an airplane taking off and knew her father could be in the cockpit, the instruments in front of him as familiar as his own face. As frightened as she was, she had to believe that he knew their sequence, that he understood their reactions and could reckon with their gauges. The plane became part of him, the panel was an extension of his mind communicating with the new and powerful body he had assumed, lifting its heavy wings against the wind, urging it through clouds, directing it to a black spot on his map. Suddenly she knew it was somehow the same with Taylor.

She dropped to the bench and shut her eyes. The frantic, excited noise of the crowd engulfed her. Spectators were shouting for different cars, names she didn't know, drivers who probably meant something to them —husbands, friends, sons, brothers. Only Dwayne's voice came out of the roar at her. "Looka there! Hey boy, look!"

She was being pulled to her feet and she opened her eyes to see the Mercury slide into the curve. It straightened itself miraculously and took a tenuous lead over a white Plymouth that was taking a rut closer to the inside.

"Taylor's ahead!" Dwayne yelled to the crowd. "That's Taylor's car!"

The track was short—only a quarter of a mile—but when Taylor was on the backstretch and lost to her in the dust, Casey sat down again and looked over at Gwen, who had come to life and was sitting up, her bare legs swishing on the windshield like a set of nervous wipers. She had put on sunglasses with red plastic frames and she held her ponytail off her neck with one hand while she slapped a frantic rhythm on the car with the other.

"He's winning!" Dwayne yelled. He bounced on the rickety bleacher and flung his arms in the air victoriously. "See that!" he yelled to the crowd. "He's winning!"

"Eight laps to go," Casey said.

Thick gray dust rose in front of them as wheels churned the dirt track. The cars were beginning to show abuse, their gleaming numbers dulled by dust, their paint jobs splotched and revealing dents and rust beneath their wax.

"He's gettin' 'em!" Dwayne shook his fist toward the track. "He's getttin' 'em good!"

Casey pulled at Dwayne to sit down, but he ignored her. Caught in the spirit of the event, he slapped himself and bounced on the bleachers, screeching instructions to Taylor and railing at the opponents.

"Look out!" he shouted. "He's coming on!" A car in the middle of the pack slung itself at the back of a Ford, trying to gain a position on the inside. The car under attack caught the blow on its rear, and like the recipient of a swift kick, lunged across the little ditch and into the infield where it banged into a parked pickup and settled down, its front squashed into the side of the empty truck.

"Oh, Jeez!" Gwen yelled, jumping off the car. "Look at that!" she called to Frankie, who was standing on the bed of the truck next to her. "That's my brother's truck! Look at that! Jeez!" She put her hands on her hips and studied the wreckage. "He was going to sell it," she wailed at Frankie. "He was going to sell that truck and the race car, too, and invest in a rig. He was gonna start hauling up into Virginia. We were gonna get rich, dammit. And now look!"

She stamped back to the car and hoisted herself onto the hood, where she stood up to see into the infield better. "Eason Warfield!" she yelled. "What you gonna do now, huh?"

The cars were coming around again.

"Fifth lap," Casey whispered.

The driver was crawling out of the smashed Ford. The audience gave him a little round of applause, although their attention had already returned to the possible winners. The Plymouth had overtaken Taylor on the last corner and it zoomed into the seventh lap half a length ahead of him. Now the same Chevy that had bumped off the Ford edged up on him, vying for second place.

"Watch out!" Dwayne yelled. "He's coming! He's a-comin' on!"

They went into the ninth lap with the three cars tailing each other like they were stuck, but in the turn the Plymouth lost a tire. The missile spun into the air, hit the top of Taylor's Mercury, and bounced off in front of the Chevy. The last car skidded into the loose rubber, maneuvered crazily around it, and straightened up within a breath of Taylor, who was trying to avoid the tireless wonder in front of him.

"They're gonna crash!" Dwayne roared.

Casey shut her eyes, closed her mind, stood suspended in the silence that overpowered the slamming of metal she refused to hear.

"*Wow-weeeeeee!*" Dwayne yelled.

Casey opened her eyes to see the Plymouth on its side against the fence and, in the backstretch, a screen of dust under which she could only hope Taylor and the Chevy were still battling. "What's happening, Dwayne?" she asked.

"He's winning. I knew he would! He's running good!"

Casey focused on the finish line, saw the flag waving, and then the green car screeching to a halt in front of them. The Mercury sat there in the dust as if stunned itself. It was quiet. The other cars passed around it and began pulling off the track.

The loudspeaker seemed to be belching on the dust. Every other word was lost in a giant swallow. "The ——ner ——lor Flan——gan. Driv—— a for-ty —— Merc—ry. Big hand —— Taylor Flan——gan!"

The crowd was cheering. Taylor might not be their husband, boy friend, cousin or brother, but he was the winner. He crawled out of the car, his body and clothes covered with a film of grime, disfigured by smudges of sweat and grease, looking inhuman.

He grinned up at the stands, acknowledging the crowd and shaking the trophy someone had slipped under his arm.

"I was supposed to give him that trophy!" Gwen shouted at them. "They told me I could be the one to do that!" She was jabbing her finger at the track manager, who grinned at her and shouted back, "You can give him something else, I reckon!"

The crowd laughed, but Gwen ignored them.

"It's hot out here, Taylor," she said, as if the rest of

the field wasn't listening. "You go on and get cleaned up so we can get outa here."

"She's wanting to go!" someone in the stands yelled down to Taylor.

"Yeah, she's *hot!*" another man laughed.

"I'm going," Taylor called. "Frankie, come help me get the car outa here." He dropped the trophy through the window into the seat and wiped his face with his sleeve.

"Hey boy!" Dwayne yelled. "Me and K.C.'s here!"

Taylor squinted into the stands.

"We come to see you win!" Dwayne called. "And we seen it!"

"Who's that, Taylor?" Gwen yelled, pointing at Casey and Dwayne.

"I'll meet you all at the gate," Taylor said. "All three of you!"

Gwen gave Casey a haughty look and slipped off the car. She stood there a minute, stretching her arms over her head with her stomach sucked in and her bottom pinched tight. Then she walked over to them. "I got to change clothes, too," she said. "I'm going to supper at the Flanagans' house tonight."

"So am I," Casey said. She was looking down into the halter top. "We'll see you at the car," she said, pulling Dwayne in the other direction.

"Wait a minute," Gwen called after them. "Who are you?"

"Casey Flanagan. Taylor's my uncle."

"Your uncle? You're kidding me. Taylor's not a uncle!" It struck Gwen hard that she had another Flanagan to cope with. She didn't like to think about

Taylor's having relatives at all. She didn't want anyone getting in the way of her having him just the way she wanted him, complete with a lumber business and a 1950 Chevrolet.

"Sure he is. I live with him, too." Casey was enjoying Gwen's obvious discomfort. "See you later."

"Wait a minute," Gwen said, edging closer to the bleachers. "Come here."

Casey leaned down so her face was close to Gwen's. She could see black bits of mascara sticking to her lashes and a little round blister of a pimple under the melting makeup on her cheek.

"Who's that with you?" Gwen whispered.

"He's all right. He's our neighbor, Dwayne Pickens." Casey tried to give Gwen a secretive look. "There's just one thing, though. He thinks I'm a boy."

"He what?" Gwen stretched her neck to get her ear closer to Casey's mouth. "He's crazy, isn't he? You tell me the truth now. I'm not going off with some crazy."

"He wouldn't hurt a fly," Casey said, "unless of course it was the person who told him I'm a girl. He doesn't like girls so that would probably get him riled up."

"Well-l-l." Gwen was backing off. "I reckon I'll see you at the gate in a few minutes." She slung her bag over her shoulder and gave them a little wave. "Goodbye, Mr. Pickens."

"You hear that?" Dwayne asked with an embarrassed grin. He slapped his cap on his leg and rolled his head. "She called me Mr. Pickens. Who ever heard of such?"

"Come on," Casey said. "Taylor's going to be waiting." She dropped to the ground behind the stands and headed for the gate.

"Can't we see another race?" Dwayne called. He jumped down and was stumbling after her. "Hey, K.C.! Can't we stay? Hey boy! Boy, can't we?"

Casey looked into the crowd expecting to hear someone correct him but nobody took notice of them. She turned around to watch him coming through the people who milled around the concession stand. He seemed so oblivious of the jostling cups of soda, the popcorn bags clutched in the crooks of arms, the obstacles in his path. Maybe he'd never seen any obstacles. Maybe there was no fear in him, no wariness.

Casey felt like a mother watching her child come to her. She could see in his face his one intention. He wanted only to reach her, a stranger already familiar to him. He was at her side, and she wanted to take his hand and make a pronouncement of her pride or at least say something about their being friends but she couldn't.

So they walked along, he bounding with excitement about the race, his arms flinging as he recounted the event that filled his mind, while she, subdued with the initial reality that he was truly a child, bent her head as the question just born in her mind spread like an anxious fever. How long could he exist this way? How long would the world, even a world as small as his, allow a full-grown man to be a boy?

· 7 ·

Half past six found
them waiting at Jane Flanagan's supper table while
she forked cornbread out of bubbling oil and called to
her husband to bring on the baked fish, a gigantic shad
she'd smothered with onions, bacon, and potatoes, then
doused with butter and milk.

Ben carried the dish into the dining room, the steam
wafting into his face, and set it down at his end of the
table. Then he sat down himself, his glasses misty with
steam, and saw, through his two circles of fog, the faces
around his table.

He knew Taylor had won his race that afternoon,
although there had been no mention of it. He could tell
by the way Taylor speared his boiled shrimp, popping
them into his mouth greedily because victory had left
him euphoric and believing for the moment that anything he wanted to do, even abandoning manners at
his mother's table, was all right. Like inviting this girl
to supper. He would have had second thoughts about
bringing her if he hadn't won the race. He would have
noticed she wasn't dressed properly, that the bare arms
and shoulders her sundress exposed were hot and dry
with sunburn, and that she had an uncouth twang to
her speech that was made more noticeable by Pansy's

proper enunciation and everyone else's silence. She was quite a talker, this Gwen, although being at the table seemed to have subdued her a little. She was quiet now, and watchful, maybe even a little apprehensive. Well, she had reason to be, although she and Jane had barely exchanged hellos as yet, so the girl didn't know what she was up against.

Ben speared a shrimp of his own and looked farther down the table at his granddaughter. She looked a little rosy herself. His guess was she'd been to the races, too. If he wasn't mistaken he'd seen her with Taylor when he hauled the Mercury into the lumberyard this evening. It looked like Casey and Dwayne Pickens in the back seat of Taylor's Chevy and this Gwen what's-her-name in the front.

Jane had told him about Casey and Dwayne, how the girl was letting him think she was a boy. He knew Jane was worrying about it, but he was trying not to. After all, what was the child supposed to do all summer? Well, she didn't seem to be wasting any time finding something. Two days with them and she'd already struck up an acquaintance with the village idiot and gone all the way across town to the racetrack with him. Ben smiled a little, chewing his shrimp. He was glad she was a spunky kid, more like Jane than Jane would be wanting to admit.

"Here's the bread—finally," Jane said, thrusting the plate onto the table. "I don't know what took it so long. Let's have the fish now while it's still hot," she urged. "Pass your plates down to Ben. There's the spoon, dear. Aren't you having any shrimp, Hazard? I thought you loved shrimp. Why, I fixed them especially with you in mind."

Hazard poked at his cocktail, got up a tiny shrimp and dropped it into his sauce, where he left it drowning.

"He doesn't seem to have much appetite," Pansy said, as if he weren't there or else were a child to be talked about.

"Off your feed, huh?" Taylor chuckled. He crammed the last of his shrimp into his mouth and sent his plate down the table to his daddy. "Well, I'm starving."

"How about you, Casey? Ready for fish? Pansy? Gwen? You look about ready to me." Ben dished buttery sauce over Taylor's fish and sent it back to him.

Gwen was picking at her shrimp. She didn't like seafood. Who would have thought it, her first and maybe only dinner at the Flanagans' and they had the one thing she couldn't swallow? Why, they could have had pig's feet and she'd have eaten. They could have had chitterlings or hashlet and she would have forced them down. But fish! What was she going to do? Her plate went down to Taylor's father and came back steaming with a rich, raw odor. The potatoes, she decided anxiously, her face and neck flush with indecision. I'll eat the potatoes. Avoid the onions where I can. And fork around the fish.

"I declare, I think I'm losing my mind," Jane said, heading back to the kitchen. "I forgot the shad roe and eggs."

Oh, God, Gwen thought helping herself to an adequate amount of cole slaw. Roe! What could that be?

The bowl Jane brought in passed under her nose. It looked like scrambled eggs speckled with brown globs. She'd seen something like that once before, but where? She put a tiny bit on her plate. The smell—Lord, it was rotten—whiffed into her face. It smelled like the caviar she'd tasted once at her rich second cousin's wedding reception. It was fish eggs. They expected her to eat fish eggs! Well, she wouldn't. She couldn't.

She felt like crying. No, she was afraid she was going to cry. What if she did? What if, when everything was going just the way she wanted it to—Taylor had won the race and finally invited her to meet his parents, even have supper with them, when she thought there was a chance she could be his special girl friend, maybe even marry him someday—what if now, with everything so nearly perfect, she went all to pieces over fish eggs?

Well, she wouldn't. She just wouldn't. She lifted her napkin to her lips, then pressed it under her eyes to make sure her mascara wasn't running. Her insides were crying even if she wasn't. Her eyes felt watery and her throat tight. She stifled a little moan, thinking how she needed to repair herself, heal the damage she felt she'd already done by not liking seafood. Why did she have to be born hating fish?

At the other end of the table, Jane was watching Pansy and Hazard, having determined earlier in the evening to avoid thinking about this girl Taylor had brought home. She'd have plenty of time for that. Besides, she wanted to give this girl a chance. No snap judgments this time. No subtle discouragement. At least she was pretty. That blond hair probably wasn't natural, but what did that matter? A lot of young women were peroxiding their hair nowadays. It didn't mean anything.

Hazard looked pained. He was toying with his fish, not eating any more than Gwen was. Like two people

in love, Jane thought, and then paused in her thinking
to look at Hazard seriously. Why, he *was* in love! Who
said he couldn't lose his appetite and get weak-kneed
just like anybody else? Well, here she was middle-aged
and so set in her ways, she was almost past believing
that people of her generation could fall in love. Romance seemed so frivolous to her now. Well, it shouldn't.

She knew she was still in love with Ben. *In love.*
That was what she meant, although she'd have a hard
time saying it, even to him. It was so much easier just
to say she loved him. After all, she had spent years loving him, taking care of him. Her dedication to him and
their sons had consumed her, energized her, probably
even aged her, but still she was in love with him, could
feel giddy when she looked out from the church choir
to see him looking back at her, loving her over the distance of straight-backed women and drowsy, nodding
men. There was a way he had of smiling at her that
conjured up his look thirty-five years ago when they
were courting and he'd come bounding onto her daddy's
front porch as if he'd been coming all day long, every
movement and thought at the lumberyard nothing more
than another step toward nightfall and being with her.
Good heavens, what a feeling that was, knowing someone thought about you all the time like that. Somebody
cared about you that much.

She looked from Hazard to Pansy, these apparitions
at her table. They surprised her a little, accustomed as
she was to their ordinary behavior, their dependable
combination of antics and solemnity. She'd been just as
surprised when she'd walked down the street earlier today to ask Pansy to supper and had found her in her
bathrobe, still at her morning coffee at ten o'clock.

"I feel so lazy," Pansy had said by way of an apology. "Come on and have some coffee with me." She hadn't even combed her hair, and there was a sleepy, drugged blush on her face. Jane thought she looked very innocent, very young, as if time had moved differently for them during the night, and daylight had found them years apart.

They had sat across from each other as they had many Saturdays before, although until today always at an earlier hour—eight thirty when Jane's men were off to work and Pansy was just up from her laziest morning of the week, the only day she didn't begin at six thirty.

Pansy had always gotten up with her father. Made his breakfast and tidied the kitchen before meeting him at his office at nine. By then he'd done rounds at the hospital and made house calls while she'd dusted the parlor or gardened a little and then spent a few precious minutes soaking in the tub, taking sweet advantage of the silence in her house. She liked being alone. She liked the aroma of bath oil and soap on her steamy bathroom walls. She liked being barefooted and robed in her kitchen, having the last of the coffee before putting on the stiff girdle that held her body in place by clamping wrinkles into stationary folds. And then selecting an outfit from among the shirtwaist dresses and soft skirts and blouses on which she wore her mother's jewelry—brooches, a delicate double strand of pearls, a cameo of peachy stone set in fine spun gold. She liked to wear the colors of roses, lilacs, peaches, plums. It pleased her skin to hover close to summer fruit and flowers. It made her happy to look through the closet, eyeing her one extravagance, searching for the perfect color to suit her mood.

In the doctor's office, amidst his antiseptic white, she was like a flower to admire, a hothouse fruit ripe for the picking, as she wrote numbers in her ledger books, accepted payments, wrote down appointments, listened kindly to complaints she'd trained herself to barely hear, much less remember.

She liked the figures in the ledger, even the perfectly lettered names she drew in the appointment book, but she didn't really like the people they represented. The people were sick. They coughed at her and left dirty tissues in her wastebasket. They handed her ancient bills from out of their soiled pockets. They had ringworm, strep throats, urinary tract infections. They sat stiffly on aching, arthritic bones and came too slowly when she beckoned them into the examining room.

It wasn't that she wasn't sympathetic, or even sometimes felt heart-wrenching pity. She did sometimes, against her better judgment. Sometimes, when all else failed, she consoled a sobbing child with a penny candy from her pocketbook or offered her arm to a frail body that shuffled weakly across her slick clean floor. But she didn't like to, didn't want to. She believed she did her job efficiently, even kindly, but she didn't want to care about those people. Once she started, where would the limit be? She was no nurse, it was not her inclination. That part of her life that needed a recipient of her care would simply have to go unfilled, unless, of course, Hazard Whitaker took it upon himself to fill it. And yesterday, he had done just that.

The two women studied each other over their cooling coffee.

"Taylor's bringing this Gwen person home for supper tonight," Jane said. "I thought you and Hazard could be with us, too, unless you've already planned something."

They sipped their coffee, each wondering how they could grab hold of the other. They had been friends for so long, as long as either of them could remember, but there had never before this been any apprehension between them, no fear that what they said to each other could do irreparable damage to their affection, no inhibitions that kept them from speaking the truth.

"Nothing has been planned," Pansy said tearfully. She got up suddenly, holding her mauve housecoat close to her breasts, and turned to the coffeepot on the stove although both of them still had full cups. "More?" she asked with her back to Jane.

"No." Jane studied Pansy's back. The housecoat made her seem taller and leaner than she really was. It camouflaged her softness, barricaded her openness with a wall of tightly woven defenses. Against what?

"What is it, Pansy?" Jane asked.

"I don't know." Pansy put her hands up to the coffeepot as if to warm herself, but she didn't touch it. "We didn't make any plans. That's all. First I didn't want to. I felt afraid to talk about it. I was afraid I'd just imagined his wanting to marry me. Last night was somehow magical, don't you think? I couldn't help thinking I'd created him, you see, and so I could make him say whatever I wanted him to." She paused and turned back to Jane. Her face was pale, stricken with her spoken fear. She smiled sadly. "Then after we came here and were sitting on the porch, I wanted to talk about it, but Hazard didn't. He said he had to go, and I didn't see any way to keep him, so he went. Not that I minded very much. I went straight to bed and slept. But now this morning, I feel so panicky, like I can't bear to ever face him again. What if he's changed his mind, Jane? Or what if, when I see him, I know I don't want to marry him. My life is so set, you know. I've been alone all these years. What if I don't really want Hazard living in my house? What—"

"What if," Jane interrupted, "when Hazard comes down here about lunchtime, as he will probably do, he finds you in your bathrobe, uncombed, unwashed, drinking cold coffee? What will he think then?" She laughed and thumped the table. "None of your questions are more serious than that one, Pansy," she continued, seeing the strain between them broken. There was no permanent barrier between them. Not yet. "Of course Hazard meant what he said. Everybody heard him and he was speaking from the bottom of his heart. I'm sure of that. As for plans, there's plenty of time. Start making some today—it'll give you something to talk about. And as for your not wanting anybody in this house, the truth is you've always had Hazard here, in your mind, at least. Why, these cups we're drinking out of, you bought because you thought he'd like them, not to mention the new parlor drapes and your daddy's chair you had reupholstered in that fine blue material. I never noticed blue being your favorite color."

She got up and put her arms around Pansy. It was an easy gesture, grateful acknowledgment that their friendship need not be hampered by Pansy's new situation. They embraced freely, with relief and pleasure, like comrades after an arduous journey. Then they stood arm in arm.

"You come to supper," Jane said.

"I will." Pansy felt herself tremble and then Jane squeezed her arm gently. "I suppose it's all said now, Jane."

"Maybe so, maybe not." Jane let her go. "It would be silly to remind you that anything worth doing is a little bit hard. We're neither of us children who need things like that explained to us. And yet, sometimes, I have to tell myself—like when I got Casey down here with all the responsibility that involves. When we commit ourselves to something important, like a child or a marriage, we have to realize all over again that it won't all be easy. And then we have to decide not to let that hinder us. Loving is truly the biggest risk a person can take, and the one that's the most worth it."

JANE CLOSED her eyes as if to clear her vision and opened them again to find herself in her own dining room and looking at Pansy, who was pressing her napkin to her lips to signify the completion of the meal.

"We'll have the pie later," Jane heard herself saying. "Out on the porch."

They were stirring. Taylor leaned back in his chair, rubbing his stomach and sighing. "Terrific, Ma."

Gwen had pushed her uneaten dinner away, as if she refused any responsibility for it. She smiled at Jane. "It was a good dinner," she said carefully. "I enjoyed it."

Not completely ill-bred, Jane thought, giving the girl a smile. Of course, the test would be if she offered to help with the dishes. Jane stood up and began collecting plates. "Now you all go on out on the porch where it's cooler. I'll be along in a minute."

"Let me help," Gwen said, grasping two crystal goblets by the stems as if she intended to squeeze them to pieces for fear of dropping them.

"Thank you, dear, but I can manage. You go on out with Taylor now and have a good time. Casey and I will do the dishes tonight."

Casey grimaced and took the goblets Gwen gratefully released to her. Gwen didn't think she could have stood the small talk women always got into over the kitchen sink. Dirty dishes and greasy water always seemed to release the kind of determined domestic chatter she abhorred. Family talk. Babies, deaths, illnesses. Depressing subjects, enough to give a person indigestion, if, of course, they'd eaten anything, which she hadn't.

She hoped Taylor would offer her a hamburger or something on the way home, or maybe the pie they were having later would tide her over. She didn't really want to stay through the pie. She wanted to be alone with Taylor even though her shoulders were burning like somebody'd set a match to her. She lifted her arms to pull free the tight hot skin cutting across her shoulder blades. Thank God, she'd worn this sundress with spaghetti straps. She'd have just died in anything else. She shuddered, imagining what a bra would be like on her back. She could feel Taylor's hand at her waist.

"Let's go then," he was saying. "Out of the way, girl."

They followed Mr. Flanagan and Hazard through the dining room and onto the porch, leaving the women and Casey with the kitchen.

"You go on out, too, Pansy," Jane said. "I'll call you to bring out some iced tea and the pie in a little while. You go on out there with Hazard now. Keep Gwen company. I declare, she looks like a little lobster with that sunburn. Maybe you can recommend something she could put on it."

Pansy did as she was told. It was easier than thinking for herself to follow Taylor and Gwen out onto the dark porch and sit down in a rocker between Hazard and Ben while the young couple took the swing. She could see Gwen settling close to Taylor and she considered mentioning the girl's sunburn, but she didn't. What did she care about Taylor's girl friend when Hazard was here rocking next to her? It was he she was supposed to take care of, not some racetrack girl who picked at her food and didn't insist on helping with the dishes. She reached over and took Hazard's hand, patted it gently, then rested it again on the arm of his chair.

What was that for? Hazard wondered. Maybe Jane had told her that Ben had given him a job at the lumberyard. Maybe it was a condolence that he'd had to ask his best friend for work. He sighed and rested his head on the back of his chair.

He could hear Taylor and Gwen whispering to each other. How could they have so much to say? They barely knew each other, he could tell that, and here they were chattering away. Hazard cleared his throat in anticipation of saying something to Pansy, but no ideas came to him.

Ben had lit his pipe and the cherry-flavored tobacco smoke hung in the summer night. "Do you remember the time we went fishing up Leggett Creek, Hazard?" he asked softly.

"Yeah." Hazard moved in his chair, setting himself to remember.

"I caught that shad long as a man's forearm. Remember that, Taylor?"

"Yes sir, I sure do, Daddy." The swing creaked.

"It was delicious," Pansy remembered. "As good as tonight's."

"I thought everything in the good old days was supposed to be better," Taylor chuckled.

"That's what some folks would lead you to believe," Ben said. "But we know better, don't we Hazard?"

Hazard sighed a noncommittal reply.

"Nothing is better than right now," Ben said, "give or take a few things like having David here with us and there being a cool breeze stirring. You won today, did you, Taylor?"

"Yes, sir."

Through the screen door Casey saw them like shadows that moved tentatively, mysteriously, catching light on her grandmother's porch. Their voices came to her in whispers as she leaned against the jamb, her head bent to the screen as if she believed she must hear a secret word of invitation if she were to open the door and disrupt their contemplations, cause shifting bodies and cleared throats to greet her. She didn't see a place for herself out there.

An aching kind of loneliness enveloped her. She looked up, wanting to recognize these shadowy forms that she knew held such a tenacious grip on her twelfth summer. Taylor and his girl friend on the swing, cuddling in the dark with their heads together and Taylor's finger tracing a soft line on Gwen's shivering arm. Pansy, sitting still and prim in her rocker, reasoning with herself that tonight when Hazard walked her home, everything would be different. Hazard slouching, his legs extended so that his feet rested on the porch rail, clicking his fingers on the arm rests, hoping someone would break the silence and fill the night with idle conversation to relieve him of that burden. And her grandfather, drowsy with a full stomach and his pipe, half listening for sounds from the kitchen, always wanting to know that Jane was about and taking care of things.

Casey ran her hand down the door frame until she reached the cool metal latch and pushed gently against it.

"That you, Jane?" Ben asked into the darkness.

"It's me, Grandpa."

"Casey."

She heard him sighing and knew the sigh was not one of disappointment but of contentment.

"We're glad you're here, Casey," her grandfather said.

And Casey gave the screen one determined shove and went out.

8

The house positively reeked of wedding plans. Ben Flanagan said it was a smell that held an uncanny resemblance to the odor of funeral flowers long after the body had been laid to rest.

"Too thick and sweet for healthy folks to breathe in," he added as he and Casey headed home from the lumberyard. It was dinnertime and Casey had been to fetch him, having nothing better to do since Dwayne had not appeared on the back porch that morning.

"Now that the date is finally set—the seventh of July, I believe they said—we'll just have to put our endurance to the test. Are you up to two weeks of frenzy, I ask you, because those women intend to squeeze every ounce of emotion into this occasion they can possibly muster? It's been a long time coming, and Jane, for one, has a whole lot of energy saved up for it. Only thing that could top it would be Taylor's getting married. What do you think about Gwen, anyhow?" Ben gave Casey a sly sideways glance that told her he knew she and Dwayne Pickens had spent the past two Saturdays at the racetrack.

"Oh, I don't know," Casey said. She slapped a crepe myrtle bush beside the sidewalk and came away with a handful of purple blossoms. "She's all right, I guess. She works at the candy counter in the five and dime, you know. Dwayne and I went in there one day last week and there she was, big as life in a little white jacket, scooping up chocolate-covered raisins. Dwayne wanted to buy something just to let her know we were there and saw her, and she smiled and called him 'Mr. Pickens.' Now he wants to go in there every single day and buy popcorn and M and M's. I guess her being Taylor's girl friend makes her O.K. with him." Casey let the crushed blossoms in her fist fall slowly, leaving a tiny trail behind her. She brushed her hand on her jeans.

"How long do you think you can fool him, Casey?" Ben asked.

"Until he doesn't care anymore," Casey replied.

"That time might never come, honey," Ben said. He wanted to touch her arm, but her body seemed suddenly stiff and defensive. She was tense just the way David's shoulders used to be when he felt himself about to be pressured into a parental point of view. "Casey, you don't know Dwayne very well. Nobody does. How can we when he doesn't know himself? But I believe he won't take to being duped anymore than you or I would. I know you think he wouldn't pal around with you if he knew you're a girl. I suspect you're right about that because he's always been kind of heated on the subject. People bait him about girl friends and such and that sort of thing embarrasses him. But it might just be that you're not giving him a chance to like you for who you are." He paused while Casey strode ahead, not wanting to listen. "Just think about it, Casey. It's something you've got to decide for yourself."

She hurried along in front of her grandfather, knowing she was being both rude and ungrateful. After all, the family had sworn to keep her secret and she knew they would. Even Gwen, who didn't seem very smart but who was at least half scared of Dwayne. And even Pansy, who was too involved with getting married to be giving any thought to the two of them.

Well, maybe she would tell him, Casey reasoned. After all, she had the wedding to contend with. She hadn't brought a single dress with her from home, but that didn't mean her grandmother was going to let her go to the wedding in pants. Maybe she could arrive in pants and put on some sort of skirt after she got there. Dwayne wouldn't be at the wedding, anyway. She'd checked the guest list to make sure, although she hadn't expected Pansy to include a crazy person in her wedding in the first place. She was hardly consenting to invite the people Jane thought were absolutely essential.

"You're not getting married but once," she'd heard her grandmother saying to Pansy, "and these people are your friends. They've known you all your life and they expect to be invited to your wedding, Pansy."

"I'm sure they do," Pansy had retorted. "They want to see it finally done so they can gloat." She was emphatically marking through names on Jane's list with a fountain pen. "Every one of these people has tried to fix me up with a man some time or the other. They've had me to dinner, to concerts, to picnics, to every social occasion you can imagine, with me so trusting and unaware every time that they had also invited what they called an eligible man who generally turned out to be a dottering idiot or else a widower with a mournful face who expected a continuation of his comforts at my expense.

They want to be there all right, but I shan't give them the satisfaction of a freak show. I shan't be the main attraction for them to *ooh* and *ah* over, while they're saying 'It's about time' under their breaths." She studied the list now disfigured with heavy black lines. "Well, that leaves about twenty people."

"But Pansy, this is just ridiculous, not to mention terribly embarrassing! These people consider themselves your friends, whether you do or not," Jane pleaded. "They expect to be invited. They want to help you and Hazard celebrate. And besides," she added solemnly, "if you're eliminating people who invited you to supper unawares, you best eliminate me. Don't you remember how you met Hazard in the first place?"

"Of course I remember," Pansy said. She patted Jane's hand to soothe the upset she was causing. "It was my regular Thursday night because Daddy was at his supper meeting. I remember that after we ate, you and I went on to choir practice just like always. Oh, how I wanted to stay on the porch that night! I remember I almost suggested that we skip choir practice since you had a guest and all, but I couldn't bring myself to say it. It was admitting too much. I was embarrassed to death just thinking it."

The two women sat beaming at each other.

"It seems like yesterday," Jane said softly.

"Yes." Pansy's smile faded. "But it wasn't. It was twenty-five years ago and over the years that followed, I've been harassed, Jane, truly harassed. By good intentions, I'm sure, but I can't condone them now. And I can't be putting on a show that makes them think they were right—that I really did want to get married all those years. Because it wasn't that way. I was never really sure I wanted to marry anybody, not even Hazard, until the moment he asked me. I've been happy alone, Jane. I've liked my life. I could have gone to my grave not married and known I'd had a good life."

Casey couldn't help thinking, when she remembered all those conversations she'd heard between her grandmother and Pansy, that there were more retarded-acting people in their neighborhood than just Dwayne Pickens. It was a secret kind of stupidity, but as childish and emotional in private as Dwayne's was in public.

People in love acted dumb, anyhow. Pansy and Hazard were proof of that, all the time smiling at each other like they had a secret between them when the truth was as plain as the grin on Hazard's face.

He looked just like Billy Pierce did that one week he was in love with Casey in the fourth grade, mooning around behind her and stumbling over his feet like she was eventually going to acknowledge his existence and even turn a smile his way. Which she never did. And so he gave up and faded into her classroom faces, although she knew both of them remembered. It was a good memory, too, without the embarrassment that had accompanied the event itself. That was how Pansy would remember her wedding, Casey thought, no matter who attended it. She would remember that she had been special to somebody, and there wasn't any better feeling than that.

She heard the metallic slap of the baseball slamming against the drum and ran farther ahead of her grandfather. "Dwayne! Hey!" she shouted toward the lot behind the trees. "Dw-ay-ne!"

She saw him pause on the mound and then watched while he scooped up something from the ground, jumped the fence, and trotted across the street with a package under his arm.

"Hey boy! Hey, I got you a present! Guess what I got you! Betcha can't guess!" He had arrived at her side and was pointing at the package wrapped in brown paper. "Betcha can't guess in a million, trillion years what I got in there."

He was grinning. Casey thought she'd never seen him so happy, not even at the racetrack or when he'd thrown Duke Snider out at third. Still she couldn't help feeling embarrassed.

"You shouldn't be getting me a present," she said. "It's not my birthday or anything."

"That don't matter," Dwayne said, undaunted by her lack of enthusiasm. "It's a real good present, the best present I ever bought anybody." He thrust the package into her hands. "Open it up, boy! Let's see it!"

Casey tore the paper away from the taped edges and let it fall as she stood staring at the gift in her hands. It was the most beautiful baseball glove she'd ever seen.

"It's a fielder's glove," Dwayne yelled, as if he were as surprised as she. "It's a fielder's glove, Mr. Ben," he called to Casey's grandfather, who was coming up behind them. "I went down to the hardware store this morning and I says to Mr. Wilson down there, I says, 'I wants to buy a fielder's glove,' and he says to me, 'They cost a lot of money, boy. How much money you got?' And I says, 'Ten dollars and fifty-two cents because Mama helped me count it out this morning,' And Mr. Wilson says, 'Well, that'll do her, all right.' And so I tried them all and I pounded them some and this was the best one!" He was dancing with excitement. "Hey boy, put it on! Put it on!"

Casey slipped her hand into the glove. The leather was solid and raw against her fingers as she worked them into place and then sunk her fist into the palm. Her hand was swallowed up and she worked her fingers slowly, flexing the leather. First she cradled the glove against her chest, then reached out her arm to see it better, turned her hand slowly to study the golden grain and to inspect the web stitching and the stamped signature of Ted Williams. She curved her index finger over the top of the glove and squeezed the pocket shut.

"We got to oil it," Dwayne said. "We got to loosen it up so it fits you right. Make it soft and easy on your hand so you can pick up them ground balls like they was dandelions. I tell you, that's a fine glove you got there. See, I told you I got you something good! I told you!" He pounded her on the back and then pulled the glove off her sweaty hand and put it on himself. "See it, Mr. Ben. Ain't it a fine one?" He shoved his baseball into the webbing of the glove again and again, methodically slapping the leather into shape. "We got to work it, though. Got to do some good work on it. Come on. Let's do it!"

"Casey's got to eat dinner, Dwayne," Ben said.

"I'm not really hungry, Grandpa," Casey had an urgency in her voice that made Ben want to give in to her.

"So you want me to offer your apologies to your grandmother, huh?"

"Would you?"

"It does seem like a special occasion to me," Ben said. What could one missed meal hurt? "You two go ahead then. But don't expect anything from the kitchen before supper, Casey. You know how your grandmother is about folks not eating at mealtime."

"I won't," Casey said, already starting across the street. "Thanks, Grandpa."

Ben bent down to pick up the paper they'd dropped and when he looked up again they were disappearing between the trees on their way to Dwayne's baseball diamond.

"Let's break it in some!" Dwayne called, running ahead of her. He sailed over the fence and trotted to the mound where he'd dropped his own glove. "I'll throw you some! A few light ones is all. Why, that thing swallows your hand up. You got a little hand for a boy, you know that?" He pulled his cap down closer to his eyes, bit off a plug of tobacco which he worked carefully in his jaw, then sent the ball flying in Casey's direction.

It sank into the pocket of the new glove. Casey flipped it out, curving her palm against the sting, and tossed the ball back to Dwayne, who fired another straight at her. She caught the hot missile in the webbing, then the next in the pocket, trying to alternate the stinging palm with the hot stretching fingers that still hunted a comfortable position between their stiff leather casings.

The noon sun was white around her. She wiped her arm against her forehead, blinking to see Dwayne, who seemed to shimmer beyond her like he was doing an exotic dance. She felt lightheaded, sun-struck with heat, and hungry—but she refused to quit. She couldn't let him know that her hand was on fire, that her fingers were swelling tight in the glove fingers, or that her shoulder motion seemed to rub bone against bone. The ball kept coming, and she returned it as vigorously as she could, although she knew Dwayne was not at all taxed. He was enjoying himself, congratulating himself on his purchase while Casey picked up the grounders he occasionally sent toward her and pushed herself into the hot sunny air, her head light and burning, to grasp the frequent high balls in the webbing of the new glove.

Finally she heard a voice coming through the trees. "Casey! Casey!" It was Taylor. He followed his voice across the street and into the lot. "What are you two doing?" He leaned against the fence.

"I got K.C. a good present," Dwayne said. "Go ahead and show it to him, boy. Go ahead."

He sent a black stream of tobacco juice between his teeth while Casey gratefully tugged the glove off her steaming hand. Her fingers were as red and swollen as she'd imagined and she rested them limply behind her, out of Dwayne's view.

"Mighty fine," Taylor said, examining the glove. "Mighty fine present you got there, Casey."

"Ten dollars," Dwayne said happily.

"Big spender," Taylor agreed. "Really big."

"Yeah." Dwayne grabbed the glove himself. "I got to oil it some. Loosen it up. That boy's got a little hand, you know that?"

"Yes, well," Taylor said, seeing the need to change the subject. "It's Wednesday afternoon, you know, and I was thinking what with the lumberyard closed and all, we just ought to go somewhere. I was thinking, how about the arcade? You been there yet, Casey?"

"No. What do you think, Dwayne?" she asked hopefully because she didn't want to abandon him when he'd just given her the glove.

"*Wowee!* Them machines you're talking about!" Dwayne turned his head to spit again. "Them cars to drive. *Var-oo-om!*" His face fell. "But I ain't carrying much money," he remembered. "Spent it all on that glove there."

"I've got two dollars," Taylor said. "You can play till it's gone and then we'll call it a day."

They piled into the front seat of Taylor's Chevy and went downtown to a little building that had housed a local market before the chain grocery set up business nearby. The building had been stripped of its produce bins and refrigerators and its raw ripped walls were lined with pinball machines bulging with shiny glass and blinking lights.

Casey's empty stomach rose into her chest as she stood peering at the mass of jangling, sliding slots, flashing lights, and metal pinging metal.

"What you want to try first?" Taylor asked her.

"That one!" Dwayne shouted. He was holding out his hand to Taylor. "Gimme some money."

"You got to get change from that man over there. See him at that counter making change for people," Taylor said, slipping a dollar to each of them. "Now don't race around here wasting this, you two. Watch the games people are playing the most and try them. And make sure you don't put your money in a machine that says *Out of Order*. See that sign right there, Dwayne. You'll be throwing your money away if you put it in that one."

Dwayne was nodding enthusiastically, hardly able to

contain himself until he was free to run loose in the room.

"Now I'm going down to the five and dime to see Gwen a minute," Taylor continued. "I won't be long, so you two stay right here until I get back. You got that, Casey? Right here."

Casey nodded. She didn't care where Taylor went as long as he stopped lecturing them. Nothing was more irritating than being given money and then having to hear how to spend it.

"O.K. then," he was saying. "You're all set." He could see they weren't listening to him anymore. "O.K. now. I'll see you in a little while."

Dwayne took off for the change counter, but Casey moved more slowly, wanting to take in the place, machine by machine. She still felt dizzy from having skipped lunch and having played baseball in the hot sun. The arcade was air-conditioned, and she stood in front of the blower for a minute feeling the cool breeze through her jeans on the back of her legs.

"Ain't you gonna play?" Dwayne asked. He was bobbing his head toward the machine nearest them and he jangled his fistful of coins at her. "I got the money."

He pushed a nickel into the slot and they watched the glass interior light up. The game sent a mechanical bear across the face of a woodland scene. Dwayne sighted through the rifle attached to the case and fired at the electric eye on the bear's side. The bear rose on its hind legs, glared at them, and then started down on all fours when Dwayne fired again. The bear rose again and slumped back onto the track, his light blinking. "I got 'im," Dwayne yelled. He fired again and again. The bear raised up and fell as if he were being pumped, his electric eye blinking furiously like a gaping wound until the lights went out.

"Let's do that one, boy!" Dwayne yelled over the noise of other machines. The place was getting crowded with boys off work for the afternoon. "This one!" Dwayne had arrived in front of a machine with two steering wheels. "Let's drive these cars!"

They inserted the money and watched the double-lane highway tremble. Then the landscape jerked into motion as trees spun by, rivers disappeared around the cylinder, and a little town blurred in the distance.

"Drive," Dwayne yelled. He gripped the wheel like a maniac, his jaw working, face set in dire concentration. "I'm gonna pass you!" he shouted. "Looka here, boy! I passed you. *Wooooo-eee!*"

Casey pushed hard on her accelerator and maneuvered into the lane ahead of him.

"That ain't fair," Dwayne said. "I'm gonna bump you offa this road, just like them drivers do out at the track!"

He gave her a spiteful grimace and then looked back into the machine to see his car wobbling on the road. "My car's broke!" He pressed on the accelerator with all his might but the car was coming to a gradual, defeated halt behind Casey's. Dwayne twisted his wheel angrily and let it spin back into place. "It quit," he said mournfully "Just when I was gonna beat you good!"

"Let's try another one," Casey suggested, wanting to get his mind off defeat. He seemed truly angry with her. "I've got to get some change. You go ahead and pick one. Pick a good one now."

With change in her pocket, Casey turned back to see Dwayne across the room, beckoning to her. He was playing one of the flipper games and she went to the machine next to him and inserted her coin. The playfield lit up and she snapped the lever, sending the steel ball up the shoot and into the field of thumper bumpers and bells. The ball eased through the maze, racking up points, and she worked the flipper buttons eagerly as if she were galvanized, part of the machine that sparkled and clanged with her winnings.

"I'm gonna do another one," Dwayne said and left her while she inserted another nickel to play the flipper game again.

"Over here, boy!" she heard Dwayne calling over the bells as the ball rounded the posts. "Come see this 'en!"

By the time she reached him, he had already pushed his coin into the slot and the interior of the machine had shown a faint light on a dark blue background. It was a night sky and Casey saw small lights flickering across it. They were the targets toward which Dwayne was aiming a machine gun.

"What is it, Dwayne?" she heard herself asking incredulously, although even then, at her distance, she knew what it must represent. A sky of planes. Tiny flickers of light appearing on the wingtips of animate aircraft. She knew, too, as she was rushing toward the machine and Dwayne was aiming down the sight, his finger clicking the trigger *ra-ra-ratt-t-t,* that she couldn't let him go on. She stood there, despising his inability to understand what she would mean if she told him to quit, to leave this easy victory and go back to killing bears. How could he understand? She stood behind him, unable to focus on the havoc inside the glass but looking instead at Dwayne's back, that crouched man's body leaning into his terrible task. He was so strong. His muscles moved under his khaki shirt, his arms flexed their bound-up strength. He could be a soldier, he could be any one of the thousands of men in uniform she'd seen in her life. He could have been someone who'd been to war and never spoke of it, someone who had flown beside her father, his eyes watchful for the plane that would spin out of the clouds to bring them down.

But he wasn't a soldier, no more than the plane he'd just hit contained the spattered, sinking remains of her father. It was a game, and a boy was playing it. Still, her ineptness to stop him astounded, even frightened her. She had no words to tell him her fear, the swift aching panic that had paralyzed her so that she could only stand staring at him with tears in her eyes. A boy crying in an arcade.

"Dwayne," she said softly, putting out her hand to touch his shoulder. "Dwayne."

He heard her over the din of his own gunfire and she saw that her voice, just the sound of it, must mean something to him because he released the trigger and turned to her. He knew something had hurt her and he must put all his strength into fixing it.

"My daddy flies in the war," she said, feeling her tears. She didn't want to cry. What would he think?

Dwayne was staring at her. His brain worked slowly through what he knew about this person. David's kid. The name stumbled into place. This was David's boy. David was in the war, and here was his kid in the arcade scared of something.

He wasn't sure of what. What in the arcade could scare a boy like that? He rubbed his head under his baseball cap. He could see tears in Casey's eyes. He could tell they were tears because his eyes were too shiny. Too round. Well, it was all right to cry. He'd cried when they took him to that place a few years back. Now Casey was in a new place, too, feeling maybe the same as him. If he just knew what to do about it.

"Let's don't play that game anymore," he said. "I don't like that one."

Casey wiped her face on her sleeve and came up with a dingy smear across her cheek.

"Boy, you got a dirty face," Dwayne said, handing her his handkerchief, which was permanently stained with baseball grime. He grinned, glad to be doing something for his friend.

"Thanks." Casey rubbed the handkerchief against the smear and then stuck the cloth in his hand. "You want to run those cars again?"

"I'm gonna beat you this time! I'm gonna beat you so bad! I'm gonna turn you every way but loose!"

"You don't know nothing about driving," Casey said, shivering back her tears. She headed for the steering wheels with Dwayne, but deep in her body the fear remained open and oozing. It would be as easy as Dwayne's aiming that fake machine gun, she knew. It would be that easy to have her daddy never come home, to have her life forever different.

They were still driving the cars when Taylor, Gwen in tow, found them. "Let's get outa here," he said. "Gwen's got the rest of the afternoon off and we're not spending it feeding these hungry monsters."

"We ain't spent all the money yet," Dwayne said, holding out the coins in his hand.

"We'll get a hamburger with it," Taylor said. "Anyhow, hadn't you rather do some real driving?"

"What are you intending to do?" Gwen wanted to know. She was wearing a little cotton dress with a Peter Pan collar and Capezio shoes with flowers on them. Casey thought she looked like a high school girl. Gwen twitched her ponytail and ran her hand up Taylor's bare arm. "I thought we were going somewhere, honey."

"We are," Taylor said. "And we're taking these two with us."

"Oh, Taylor," Gwen moaned. "I could be doing my hair."

"And miss teaching Casey how to drive?"

"I'm not old enough," Casey said, although the idea had an uncanny amount of appeal.

"Sure you are. You know right from left, don't you? You know stop from go, don't you? Why, I could teach Dwayne here to drive, couldn't I, Dwayne?"

"I reckon you could," Dwayne said with unexpected seriousness. "But first you teach K.C."

"Well, let's go!"

They headed across town to the lumberyard. Taylor unlocked the gate and drove in next to the little garage where he kept his stock car. He turned the Chevy around as it faced the open lot dotted with stacks of lumber.

"Ready, Casey?" Taylor said. "Come on up here."

Gwen, seeing for herself the necessity of sitting next to Dwayne Pickens, crawled angrily into the back seat where she leaned against the door, refusing to look at any of them. "If you all wreck this car, whatcha gonna do?" she asked finally, seeing that Taylor intended to ignore her for the business at hand.

He was explaining the dashboard to Casey. "Steering wheel, gears, radio, lighter."

"I know all the parts, Taylor," Casey said, wanting to get on with it now that she was in the driver's seat.

"All right. Clutch in. Turn on the ignition," Taylor commanded.

"He did it!" Dwayne yelled from the backseat. "Hey boy, you did it!"

The car settled into idle while Dwayne slapped the seat and roared and Gwen stared out the window, ignoring them all.

"Gears," Taylor said. "Reverse. Down for first. Up and over for second. Down for third. Clutch to shift. Wanna try it now?"

Casey nodded and pushed in the clutch while she eased the gear stick down to first.

"Great. O.K. Now. Start easing out the clutch and giving her a little gas. Not much now. We don't want to run into that pile of two by fours, do we?"

Casey did as instructed. All her concentration went into making the car move forward slowly and carefully. It went five yards and died.

"What happened?" Dwayne wanted to know. "Hey boy, you break this car?"

"Before long you're gonna be wheeling between the lumber like you were born on wheels," Taylor said. "This is where your daddy learned to drive. Then he taught me when I was about your age. Lord, I loved to drive. So did your daddy. But what he really wanted to do was sprout some wings. Wheels didn't go fast enough for him. Me, I like the dirt. I like the dust up my nose and the people yelling and cussin'. I like winning, too. But mostly I like trying those wheels on the track no matter what comes in front of me. Those potholes and flying tires aren't clouds you can sail through. They're obstacles. They'll put you out of business in a minute. In a second. But there's something about that, too, about it being dangerous, about putting what you can do to the test, not just against the track and the other cars, but against yourself. You know, Casey, if I could make a living at it and didn't have this lumberyard around my neck, I'd just drive."

He sighed and grinned at her, then looked back at Dwayne. Flushed with expectancy, he was awaiting his turn at the wheel. "Now let's get this baby going. Mama's gonna be wanting us for supper and it may take all night to teach Dwayne Pickens the rudiments of the motored vehicle."

9

*C*asey wore a dress.
A few days before the wedding, she walked with Pansy
two blocks east to Mrs. Lumby's to have it fitted. A
hand-painted sign, thread letters with a wooden needle
and spool attached, pointed them toward Mrs. Lumby's
front door. In her bright, hot parlor, Casey stood on a
large stool in her scratchy eyelet dress while Mrs.
Lumby squatted at her feet, her mouth tight with pins
that she briskly stuck into the fabric against the mea-
sure of her wooden yardstick. Casey had protested the
dress weeks ago, in anticipation of wearing one, but
even then she'd had a compromise in her head. She
would wear it once and then only in the church. Her
grandmother had agreed and had bought this miserable
itchy material that made her look like a baby. At least
none of her friends would see her in it.

"Your dress is two days away, Pansy," Mrs. Lumby
said through her pins. She spoke as if she were bringing
the dress from someplace far away rather than off her
own sewing machine in the kitchen. "You can try it
on, though. It never hurts to have another fitting."

Pansy disappeared into the kitchen and came back
wearing the rose dress with its raw, uneven hem and
gaping, zipperless back. The dress was the softest gar-

ment Casey had ever seen. She squirmed in her stiff blue eyelet while Pansy stood patiently, feeling the silkiness next to her powdered skin. The dress had a wide skirt and a bertha collar. Pansy's white chest rose against the collar that fell softly over her breasts and arms.

"All done," Mrs. Lumby said to Casey, dropping her extra pins into a tin box. "You can put on your clothes now. Let's look at you, Pansy."

Casey and the seamstress stood silent in the room while Pansy turned slowly, as if she were about to dance for them. She fingered the cloth of her skirt, lifting it and letting it fall back into place.

"I'm getting a hat," she said. "A big picture hat of the finest straw with fresh flowers on it. Roses, maybe, or camellias. Then some sprigs of baby's breath and fern. I'll carry a bouquet of roses and snapdragons and a white Testament I've been saving for an occasion such as this."

She was seeing the wedding. They were seeing it with her. The dress had transported them all. Mrs. Lumby stood with her hands folded across her apron as if the dress had been beautifully, miraculously finished, and Casey forgot her scratchy torment while they heard music, the organ from the Baptist Church down the street.

"I'll wear rose satin shoes and the sheerest stockings Broydan's sells, and perfume. Fragrance like rose petals."

They could see the wedding. Casey closed her eyes and was there. She saw herself slipping into the eyelet dress in the ladies room and squeezing her feet into the Mary Janes her grandmother had insisted she wear.

She could see Taylor and Gwen, Taylor in his blue Sunday suit and Gwen dressed to the teeth in a flowered dress with a lacy little jacket over it. She was wearing her Capezio shoes with a matching pocketbook and a tiny veil attached to her blond bun with silvery bobby pins.

When the wedding day arrived it was all just as Casey had imagined it. Jane and Ben were there on the front row as if they were the parents of the bride and groom, filling empty spaces in lives that had long been empty. Jane had a frantic look even though she was smiling, grateful the moment had finally arrived. She looked frazzled; she was functioning on borrowed energy and was destined to spend tomorrow in bed. Her old Sunday dress was wrinkled in the seat and her new hat leaned slightly to the side, blown there by the beginning of a summer storm.

Then Hazard in a white suit and white shoes. He came out of the Sunday school room with a grin on his face and a bounce in his walk as if he were prepared to perform the warmup while they waited for Pansy, the main attraction, to arrive. He clasped his hands in front of him trying to contain his nervous energy and winked at Casey. The organist was playing "O Promise Me." Miss Beulah Wendell, the choir soloist, began to sing. Her voice, old and thin, warbled out the notes of love while Hazard stared into space with a silly grin on his face and Casey twisted her shoulder blades against the pew, trying to get comfortable in the eyelet.

Pansy came down the aisle alone. Her roses quivered in her hand and she paused for a moment midway the church, looking at Hazard and the minister, who were both smiling encouragingly at her.

This is all for me, she thought. This is all because of me.

The idea made her suddenly so giddy that she wanted to lean against the closest pew and collect herself. As if she could, as if there were any collecting to be done. All her life she had been collected, in control, contained, even until three minutes ago when she'd been taking deep, rhythmic breaths in the vestibule, waiting for the wedding march. All her life she'd been waiting for this, not consciously because she had been truthful when she'd told Jane she'd been happy alone, yet she knew she hadn't wanted to miss this moment either, had been saving it like perfume until she'd thought its scent might have evaporated. Love unused became useless, became brittle and drawn, or vanished altogether. What if that had happened to her?

She resumed her walk, pushed forward by fear. If that were true, if she weren't capable of the love Hazard deserved, she would know soon enough. She would falter with it, drop it flat and useless between them, and they would have to deal with it. It was worth the risk. She hadn't come this far to deny the pain of risk taking.

They mumbled the vows, Hazard because he was scared, immobile with witless fear; he mouthed the words like a mute learning to speak. Pansy whispered, too, although it was not her inclination to show weakness or to falter in public. But she didn't want to embarrass Hazard by sounding more confident than he. It seemed to her that they should provide a solid if tremulous front even now, as they took their vows.

The minister was saying The Lord's Prayer. The words dropped on their bowed heads. Forgive us . . .

deliver us—words of contrition. The organ delivered them and Pansy felt Hazard's face against her cheek. Her mouth turned toward his and they pressed her bouquet between their damp trembling bodies.

DURING THE reception in the church social hall, a summer storm blew up above them and dropped its windy lashing rain onto the windows. Miss Beulah had consented to play the piano during the reception. She sat straight and serious before the yellowing keyboard, fingering tunes from her head; across the room, at the refreshment table, Jane ladled pink punch into clear cups and urged cake and finger sandwiches she'd made on the guests.

Pansy was cutting the cake herself and wiping the knife carefully on a napkin between each slice. It was a duty she enjoyed because it took some skill and care. She turned her mind to it readily, accustomed as she was to fulfilling such tasks at wedding receptions. She hardly seemed the center of attention now that an atmosphere of celebration had taken over, but she liked that. She wanted to be efficient and unobtrusive—as a good hostess should be. She smiled to herself, seeing how relaxed and comfortable everyone seemed. Even Hazard, who was drinking cup after cup of punch, quenching a day-long thirst that had dried his mouth and shriveled his stomach. He was reviving before her eyes, turning rosy with satisfaction. How he loved a party. Pansy felt grateful for having provided him with one.

It would be as easy as this, she thought, shifting a slice of cake deftly onto a china plate. She could make him happy as easily as this. Hazard had certainly never demanded much of her in the past. His pleasures were simple ones. He was a simple man.

She was the complicated one. She was the one whose passions rose to discomfort her when he seemed so calm, so unperturbed by the impending events, the hours ahead of them. Looking at him now, it was hard to remember what had attracted her to him in the first place. Oh, she remembered the events well enough, but the emotions that went with them had faded over the years, and a carefulness had filtered into her early stirrings of romance. It was good they were married, Pansy thought, and not a minute too soon. She was not, after all, old wine; more likely, a spice that could lose its savor.

Hazard was directing Casey toward the piano. Casey looked pretty in her dress. She could possibly turn into a good-looking woman when and if she filled out and had her hair curled. Pansy thought she looked uncomfortable in her dress, but not foolish. Hazard was trying to get her to sing. Pansy could tell he was urging her because he had his arm around her and she was giving him a worried, plaintive look, the look of a girl who was expected to expose herself and her talents. If she had any.

It was Hazard who said the child could sing. He'd even wanted her to sing at the wedding, but Pansy had put her foot down. No twelve-year-old tomboy, not even one in a specially created blue eyelet, was going to ruin her wedding. No, she'd have Miss Beulah, who was at least dependable.

But Hazard would have his way. She could see him working his will on Casey now, nuzzling her like a sheepdog. He was conferring with Miss Beulah, too, who seemed delighted to contribute to the entertainment.

She began to play. Hazard backed away as if to give his floor show a stage. Rain washed against the windows and a chord of thunder rumbled around them as Miss Beulah took her introduction into a high register. The old piano thundered a little as she brought it down again into Casey's range.

Casey craned her thin neck out of the raw eyelet collar and closed her eyes. She was doing this for Hazard, a gift just for him, because since that first day when he'd come into her room and danced, the light touching him in such a fantastic, magical way, she'd loved him. Loved his puny jokes, his awkward manners, his nonsensical way of dealing with things, even his age, his ancient, timeless yearnings that told her that every year of her life could bring its special joys, its moments of dancing.

She heard her own voice. It came as from her mother's body, that tender delicate throat that could sing away pain and that Casey had long ago learned to mimic.

"You made me love you . . . I didn't wanna do it . . . I didn't wanna do it . . ."

Jane stopped the ladle midair. It was Casey she heard against the summer storm outside. It was Casey in a summer dress, her patent leather Mary Janes biting her toes, her hair brown and shining like David's. She was a girl. Jane could see that. Deep inside this child, the woman she would become lived and was slowly nourishing herself on songs like this one, on words from books, on nights when she must want to hug her-self in the sheer magic of being alive and growing. A woman being born with as much pain and pleasure as being twelve could bring to anything.

"You made me want you . . . And all the time you knew it . . . I guess you always knew it . . ."

Gwen licked her lips smoothly and looked at Taylor, who was staring at his niece. What was he seeing? A transformation, that was for sure. Why, the poor thing looked half pretty in that dress even if her bony white knees did show above her socks and her hands, pressed to her stomach, were coarse and ragged-nailed. Half a tomboy was what Taylor was seeing, and he was looking at her as if he wanted to save that tomboy half, as if she was being lost to him right now while she sang those pearly notes, her thin chest pushing out her wind like perfectly tuned pipes resided there.

Well, Taylor could just turn his mind to other things. In a few minutes, they'd be out in his car going home, Gwen supposed, while Hazard and Pansy caught the train for their wedding trip, a honeymoon for old folks. Gwen wanted a honeymoon herself. She pressed her hand into the curve of Taylor's arm as if to tell him so.

"You made me happy sometimes . . . You made me glad . . . And there were times, dear . . . You made me feel so bad . . ."

Hazard looked across the room at Pansy. She seemed so far away from him, hours or miles away, like he'd felt sometimes in his room above Papa Tutoni's. But here she was, as accessible as steps were, as beautiful as he'd ever imagined anyone could be. Her hat shielded part of her face. He wished she'd get rid of it, show herself to him across the room with all those people between them. Give him some display of affection, some sign that she understood why Casey was singing, what had motivated him to put music to this event. Surely she knew it was his way of loving her. Surely she would understand . . .

"You made me sigh for . . . I didn't wanna tell you . . . I didn't wanna tell you . . ."

He wanted to dance. His feet, heavy and tight in his new white shoes, seemed to have found memory in the music. He did a slow grapevine onto the floor. He knew that if he ever danced in his life, this should be the time. Right now, with the people he loved most in the world in this room, he wanted to show them the delicate, complicated maneuvers of his art, the gifts of his childhood, his birthright. It seemed so precious a gift. He trembled against the fear that he couldn't do it justice, that his legs and feet, tired from years of dull, worthless waitering, from the waste of years, could not dance.

"I want some love that's true . . . Yes I do, 'deed I do, you know I do . . ."

He abandoned himself to it. It was the only way, the final release of all his fears that he and Pansy had foolishly let life go by and that this wedding was a sham of good intentions executed too late to save either of them. His feet were gliding, his body felt loose and agile in his skin.

"Gimme, gimme what I cry for . . . You know you got the brand of kisses that I'd die for . . . You know you made me love you. . . ."

Hazard danced.

• *10* •

*T*hey *ordered a late sup-*
per on the *Southern Crescent* headed for Washington,
although Pansy wasn't in the least bit hungry. What
she needed was the comfort of the carefully set table,
the beautiful manners of the waiter, the heavy napkin
that covered her lap like a starched white blanket, the
dull glowing silverware, the steaming dishes. Hazard
sat across from her, looking out the window as the
night flew by. The train seemed sure and swift; he
watched lights fall away into shadows as the evening
forest loomed beside the track.

"Would you care for dessert?" the waiter was asking
him, although his plate had not been touched.

"Huh? Oh, no thanks." Hazard looked at Pansy, who
was having her coffee, her eyes down as if to avoid
his stammering, his lack of appetite, his malaise.

"No, thank you," she said, resting her coffee cup
carefully. "We'll be going to the sleeping car soon."
She looked at Hazard, expecting to see him smile at
her willingness to admit the coming night between
them.

But he was out of his seat and following the waiter
down the aisle. She watched the two of them in conversation, Hazard slouching forward while the waiter

stood straight, conscious of being watched, polite but regretful.

Hazard came back slowly while Pansy pressed her napkin to her mouth. She felt the stiff starchy coating on the napkin and wanted to crumble it in her hands as if such a feeble attempt at violence would relieve the torment on Hazard's face and keep her from having to hear whatever bumbling, stupid thing he was forced to say.

"We don't have a berth," was what he said, his head hung like a culpable child's. "I forgot to reserve a berth and they're all taken."

"You mean—" Pansy started and then stopped, not wanting to say out loud what a failure he was.

"It's just six hours to Washington," Hazard was saying. "It's midnight already, so we'll be there early in the morning. We can just sit here and talk. We can—"

His own words horrified him. What was he saying? That he and Pansy, after twenty-five years of waiting, would spend their wedding night in the dining car of the *Southern Crescent* bound for D.C.?

She stood up. She couldn't stand to look at him, but where could she go?

"The lounge car, ma'm," the porter said behind her. "I can give you pillows and a blanket."

"Thank you," Pansy said stiffly, not wanting to be appeased. Why should she be satisfied with a porter's duty when her own husband had failed her so miserably? Her husband.

She turned away from him and followed the porter down the aisle, past the white cloths and deserted places, through the narrow, blowing bit of dark into the lounge car. Empty, too, except for a few men already sleeping in their chairs. Pansy knew they were men accustomed to sleeping anywhere. They would awaken at the station and go blinking into the bright morning light, their hair in stiff points where they'd rested their heads, their stubble of beards smudging their sleepy faces. They would clean up in the station lavatory, maybe even pull a fresh shirt out of their bag of wares, and then be off to sell something, anything.

She sat down in the first chair she came to and closed her eyes. Hazard was like those men. He had spent years selling things, riding trains at night to get himself to another job in the morning. A chair in the lounge had been all right for him then. But now? And for her? How could he let it be enough for her?

She sighed and rolled her head on the back of the chair. Already she was aching, weary from the tension of her wedding day. She wished she were at home soaking in her tub. She wished she could shed her girdle and loosen the covered buttons on her blouse that were suddenly digging into her backbone like blunt little nails. She wished she were in bed with Hazard Whitaker, in a berth which, even in her most fanciful imaginings, had not been an ideal situation. She had worried about the cramped quarters, the proximity of the other passengers, the knowing looks she might face in the morning. She had felt dread, but not fear.

She heard the door open and close, felt the swift cool air against her legs. She knew it was Hazard. She could feel him looking down at her, thinking probably that she was already asleep. He wouldn't know what she was feeling, what humiliation she felt that he hadn't planned ahead, that he was letting their wedding night escape like this.

She felt a blanket touching her chest. He was pressing the folds around her legs, covering her regret, her vulnerable, needful body, with cheap railroad plaid. Well, she wouldn't sleep. But she sat still, waiting for him to move away. She didn't want to look at him. She felt with a chill that made her shudder under the blanket that she never wanted to see him again.

Hazard was awake, too. He sat by the window, looking out but also looking at Pansy, who sat too neatly to be sleeping but who nevertheless had her eyes shut. She was avoiding him, making it hard for him to apologize. It was just as well, even though he was truly sorry. He was more sorry than he could ever tell her, not because they weren't in bed together, but because he had hurt her already, so soon, like he'd always feared he would. Why, he had worried himself into this mistake just like a child who spills his plate because he's afraid he will.

He stared out the window. The night was passing him by. He leaned back and propped his feet on the window ledge. Over his shoes he could see a light here and there, dotting the black, sleeping landscape. He'd spent many nights just like this—on trains or busses, although he loved trains best. They were more than just transportation, they were a way of living. Why, a man who kept a room in the worst part of town and had one suit and paper in his shoes could be as rich as cream on a train.

With a few dollars and a sandwich in his pocket, he could hobnob with the best of them, read the paper, play a little rummy, and nobody would ask him where he was going or why. The trip itself was what counted, the camaraderie of the journey, the adventure of getting there. He could look successful even if he weren't, on a train.

At least he'd always thought so until tonight. Tonight, just hours after his wedding, he was living the result of the most monstrous mistake he'd ever made—not reserving a berth. The simplicity of his dilemma astounded him.

Here she was, his wife, not five yards from him, faking sleep to avoid him while he stared out the window, seeing nothing but knowing what was out there. He had visited all those little haunts between Greensboro and Washington. He'd sold shoes and pictures and a fine line of kitchenware in them. He knew those houses, kitchens stuffy with the close heat of a winter stove, the dank hallways, the parlors with their stiff, unused furniture. He had never wanted to own one of those houses. Never in all those years had he loved his destination as much as he did the journey itself.

Maybe he was destined to always be between places, riding the bus or the rails. Maybe he wasn't supposed to have married Pansy, who was as stationary as a pedestal and, at the moment, about as cold. He could see already that Pansy didn't like the traveling part, she scorned the adventure. She'd rather be at home without a honeymoon at all. Why, once they got back she'd probably never leave it again, and there he'd be, too, stuck in that fine, uncomfortable house of hers, working eight to five at the lumberyard, falling into her routine like a mouse on a treadmill, spinning himself dizzy but never dancing. Never kicking up his heels. Never forgiven for his minor mistakes, his bumbling attempts to make that woman happy. Well, by God, they'd just see about that.

He closed his eyes just as Pansy opened hers. The tiny lights along the rim of the ceiling cast flightly little shadows on them both. She was aching. Her elbows seemed stuck to the armrests, and her hands, so long folded together under the blanket, felt glued and useless. She tossed her head against the chair to force her brain into alertness. Hazard seemed to be sleeping. Well, good riddance. She didn't want to look at him, much less talk to him. How could he have made such a mess, he the world traveler who knew every station on the eastern seaboard? How could he have failed her so?

She was looking at him whether she wanted to or not. Something about his bent head, the thin forehead turned slightly toward her, the resting jaw, forced her to look at him. He was wearing his white wedding suit and looked incongruous in the dimly lit car, like a leftover party favor.

Oh, she loved him. And tomorrow in their hotel room in Washington, she would tell him so. She would forgive him, if by then she could remember why or how she had blamed him. It would be a funny story to them some day, the kind of story that was passed from generation to generation except that they would never have children to tell it to. Still, it would be part of their memory. They would laugh about it as one remembers the funny little tragedies that bind them to others, those most revealing, gentle knots of love.

She could see the beginning of day. In an hour or so they would be pulling into Washington, a city as foreign to her as San Francisco or Madrid would be, a place as rare and wonderful as any other in which to start a new life. She nestled into her blanket and sighed. She could be happy in Washington.

ONE OF their bags was missing. They were in a taxi more than halfway across town to their hotel when she missed her smallest case, the one transporting her toiletries, which she had foolishly let out of her hand in the station.

"We'll go on to the hotel," Hazard said to the driver, "and then I'll make arrangements to retrieve it."

The tone in his voice relieved Pansy. She heard a mixture of contrition and courage and knew Hazard had determined not to disappoint her again. At the hotel he had the desk clerk phone the station and learned that a messenger would arrive shortly with the missing bag.

"You needn't wait down here with me," Hazard said and sent her up to their room behind the bellhop, who opened the curtains and the bathroom door, snapped open her suitcase, and then left her.

She would take a bath, she thought, while she waited for Hazard. But she didn't have anything but a comb, a compact, a lipstick, and of course, the soap provided by the hotel. That would do, she reasoned, and she got out her new robe of peach silk with lacy butterfly sleeves.

But what if he arrived before she was out of the tub? What if he unthinkingly rushed headlong into the bathroom while she languished in the cool clear water?

She would lock the door, both the outside door and then the bathroom door. Hazard would have the key to their room, but would he be offended to discover the bathroom door locked? The only thing to do was to take a very quick bath, just long enough to take the restless night off her skin. She sat up straight in the tub, half turned from the door, and washed hurriedly while listening for the clicking lock that would signal Hazard's arrival.

Out of the tub, she rinsed it carefully and then applied what little makeup she had with her. She put on her underwear and the peach robe and sat down to wait. She was hungry. It was almost ten o'clock, but she decided to wait for Hazard to decide about breakfast. Or would they have lunch? Perhaps they would have brunch right here in the room. Over there by the window, she in her new robe and Hazard in his—she couldn't imagine what he would be wearing. A dressing gown, perhaps? Heaven help them both, his undershirt. Well, the white suit would be better—at least she was used to it.

She read the room-service menu carefully, selecting what she would have. Half a cantaloupe with assorted melon balls, a poached egg on toast, two slices of Canadian bacon, a brioche, coffee with cream. She stood the menu back in its fold on the dresser and opened the drawer. Stationery bearing the hotel insignia, a brochure describing some of the national monuments, a Gideon Bible. She closed the drawer. She was not yet prepared to read literature designed to compensate for loneliness or to make her feel at home.

The hands on her watch slipped toward noon. Then

toward one. The day was falling away soundlessly, like the turning pages of the Gideon Bible she held on her lap. She read the words slowly, forcing herself to think about the story of Daniel because it was a better story than the one she could envision closer at hand. This lone Israelite in the lion's den made more sense to her than she did in a hotel room in Washington, D.C., husbandless, a widow on her honeymoon, deserted either by intention or fate. She didn't know which.

She closed the Bible, knowing she had to find out. If he were dead, struck down by a car while retrieving her missing bag, she must know it. And if he had left her, she must know that, too.

She put on her apricot suit again, turned her diamond wedding ring straight inside her white glove, and closed the door behind her.

He was in the bar. She could see him through the open French doors leading from the lobby where she stood, peering into the dim recesses of the room from which she heard laughter and the clink of glass on metal trays. The white suit had a dingy cast to it now, as worn as the man inside it, for Hazard had a drunken glaze over his face, a will-less, stupid expression, although he was the one laughing the loudest, swallowing boldly, slapping his hand on the table while his two companions, men in similar states, laughed at him.

She stood, turned to stone, watching him even though she couldn't believe what she saw. It was not within her realm of imaginings. She simply did not believe that the man she was seeing was Hazard Whitaker, yesterday her groom. But then he turned to her. Like a thief who sensed apprehension, he looked her full in the face, his lips loose and foolish, his eyes barely focused but nevertheless seeing Pansy in her shiny summer honeymoon suit, that flower he had picked just yesterday.

He stood up to face her. It was his intention to draw her into his party. He would introduce her to these salesmen friends of long ago. He would order her a champagne cocktail, the first she would have ever tasted, and they would toast her, the goddess rising out of their celebration squalor, the queen of his kingdom, his own true love.

But she was gone. The ghost of her lingered for a moment before his sobering eyes, just long enough to tell him he had failed her again. Somewhere growling in his gut a fear sprang up. She had left him.

HE FOUND her in the train station, her hands folded in their white gloves, her hat perched defiantly on her head, while she waited for the train to take her home. He sat down near her, but not too near, just so she'd know he was there and she wasn't alone. He had collected their bags from the room, the suitcase of her things left open so he had to touch the soft silky fabric she had folded there. It seemed wrong of him to touch her things, as if he were defiling her; he closed the suitcase quickly, wanting to close his mind too, although that proved impossible. He could see where she had been sitting on the bed, the slightly rumpled coverlet, the pillow not quite in place. She had been there alone; in this room she had waited for the new beginnings of her life like a prisoner awaiting sentencing.

Now he watched her waiting for the train. It would be all night again on the train, again without a berth, he supposed.

"Pansy," he said softly, but she didn't acknowledge him. "Pansy, I'm so sorry."

She didn't turn her head, but he could see her chin trembling and a tear slip down her cheek into her collar.

"I'll make it up to you," Hazard said, still keeping his distance. He could feel the distance. "I know you don't think I ever can, but I'll find a way. I promise."

Still she didn't see him. She pressed her handkerchief to her face. He did not exist for her anymore.

⇒ *11* ⇐

That week the National League beat the American League 8–3 in the All Star Game. Stan Musial, Bob Elliott, Gil Hodges, and Ralph Kiner all hit homers for the National. In Tucson, Arizona, the mothers of two soldiers who had died in an undeclared war in Korea were denied the Gold Star because their sons had been killed in "peacetime." Jane Flanagan bought her granddaughter the sheet music to "Tennessee Waltz." Hazard Whitaker lay in his room next to Casey's when he wasn't working at the lumberyard. Wherever he was, he was subdued and silent under the weight of whatever had happened on his honeymoon.

Dwayne Pickens took Casey to see Susan Hayward in *I'd Climb the Highest Mountain,* during which Casey slid low in her seat and put her hands on her temples so he wouldn't see her cry. He also took her to see *King Solomon's Mines,* where he announced aloud what would be happening next because he had already seen the picture twice.

Pansy went to work as usual. Dr. Kemble did not question the length of her honeymoon or the tearful expression she hid periodically behind a monogrammed handkerchief. Five cases of polio had been identified among his patients by then, one of whom was already in a Raleigh hospital, being kept alive in an iron lung. The health department was considering a proposal to close the swimming pool, the racetrack, the arcade, all the places young people were likely to congregate. Dr. Kemble hoped the situation wouldn't come to that; meanwhile, he recommended that children stay close to home. He saw them around town anyway. They had not seen an iron lung or many crippled limbs. They had not been touched yet, and he could only be grateful for that.

On Saturday, Dwayne went to cut his brother Alva's grass as he did every week. It was the house in which his parents had lived, where Dwayne had been born and spent most of his interminable childhood. He knew every splinter of that house, he knew the smell and touch of it. Standing on the front lawn, looking up at the sparkling white two-story frame, he felt an urgency to return to it, to find himself there again. His mind curled, like a baby seeking fetal position, into the familiarity of the house, the warmth of his sudden acute memory of having lived there.

Alva's wife, Marge, was at home. He could see her big white Chrysler sticking out of the garage, so he knew he couldn't get into the house. Marge had changed everything, anyway. His room had a piano in it now, and there were heavy curtains on the windows that his mama had always left bare and open to the sun he'd loved to feel warming his wood floor, his bed, the models of trains and cars his daddy used to make for him.

Now those things were in his room on Chestnut Street. His mama had brought them in boxes on a big

Chapter Eleven

truck. He had unpacked them himself, but it wasn't the same in the new house. The sun didn't strike his window the same way, and his floor had a carpet on it, and there were no stairs to race up and down.

He turned back to his task. He knew Marge didn't want him looking up at the house like that. She'd be watching him. In a few minutes, after he'd started the mower and was at the far edge of the yard, she would come out on the front porch and call to him about watching out for the flowers she'd planted. He wouldn't be able to hear her over the machine, but he knew what she'd be saying. He could mimic her and Alva because they always said exactly the same things over and over again. It was like learning a song or a radio jingle. After a while, you couldn't help but have it rolling around in your head whether you wanted it there or not.

He started the mower and cut a path from walk to hedge where there were no flowers in his way. He liked to mow the straight lines and watch the cut grass spew into the freshly cut rows. He liked the smell of gasoline and grass and the sound of the engine when it was going forward at an even speed.

He heard Marge on the front porch and he looked up at her, pulling his baseball cap lower on his forehead so she couldn't see his face. He could see her mouthing the words of warning and he nodded once and began to mow again. He could feel the sun on his back and shoulders. It had to be late morning, what with the sun so high. He'd already mowed his mother's yard because he was planning to go to the racetrack that afternoon. He was going to ride his bike out there and then find Casey, who was coming with Taylor.

Casey had explained the whole thing to him, even how they'd put his bike up on the trailer with Taylor's car and pull it home. He liked that.

"What do you think you're doing, Dwayne Pickens?" Marge was saying right in his ear. He stopped pushing the mower and looked where she was pointing. He had grazed a little yucca plant and the spikey fronds were lying in a pile behind him. He was guilty, so what could he say to her?

"Mowing," he said. He revved up the engine and pushed away from her.

She came behind him, her flowery housecoat dancing around her bare feet. "Every week I ask you to be careful, Dwayne," she said, "and every week you mow something down. What are we going to do with you?"

Dwayne kept on mowing, his face set stubbornly away from her.

"You're going to hit that azalea!" Marge yelled into his ear, pointing at the pink bush that had appeared in his path.

Dwayne mowed right into it, hitting the tiny trunk and knocking blossoms all over the ground.

"Why, you stupid moron!" Marge yelled. "You did that on purpose!" She grabbed his arm and tried to wrench him free of the mower. "Stop that thing, dammit! You stop that thing this minute!"

Dwayne pushed the gear on the bar to "Off" and the mower sputtered to a halt. "I don't like you, Marge," he said straight into her face. "You are not a nice person."

Looking into her wide angry face, he knew she didn't like him either, and her dislike was more than the momentary feeling he had toward her. He knew she had never liked him and never would. He had to think what to do, how to escape her rampage.

"It's not that we don't love you, Dwayne," Marge was saying, still holding on to his arm but having relaxed her grip, turning anger into apology. "It's just that you don't pay attention, you don't remember."

He was listening to her. She had said it before, he remembered that. He knew he could remember things. He knew Marge was wrong, and Alva was wrong, and the people who loved him were right. He knew he could remember living in that house; he could remember when the lawn was clean and dark green, left open for him to play on. He could remember how his daddy played catch with him there, and how his mama came out on the porch to bring them something cold to drink. He remembered a Christmas tree in the front window and the ice storm one winter that left a solid sheet on the walk for him to slide on. He remembered the time the porch swing chain broke and sent him sailing head first into the wall. He remembered the sunlight in his room and the car his daddy used to have. He remembered how to drive.

He pulled away from Marge and headed for the garage. He knew how to drive. Marge was coming after him, her dressing gown flapping and her hand pressed to her panting chest.

"What are you going to do?" she screamed. "Dwayne, come back here!"

The keys were in the ignition. That was something else he remembered. That was how Marge always knew where they were. He turned the key and pressed the accelerator. The engine turned over and caught.

He remembered the sound. He remembered Taylor. He remembered the repetition of his instruction. Clutch, gears, accelerate. The pattern fell into his brain like learning to tie his shoes had, because it was something he needed to do. He backed the car out into the street with Marge running along beside him skirting the shrubbery. She was screaming at him, but he had the window up and didn't try to hear her. Her face was ugly when she screamed. He remembered he didn't like her and she didn't like him.

Out of the driveway, he had to decide quickly where to go. He knew every street in town, but his mind turned toward the open road where there weren't stop signs and people, where he could get away from Marge and her screaming. He went instinctively where he would have gone on his bike—toward the racetrack, toward Casey.

Two turns and he was on the road to the fairgrounds, less than a mile away. The road was almost empty of traffic because it was still too early for the drivers to be arriving. He drove slowly, his mind repeating Taylor's instructions. He didn't have to shift now, so he concentrated on the wheel. It was such a little thing to have such power. Why, with the turn of his wrist he could cross the white line where the cars coming toward him traveled. He knew enough not to do that. He felt the control in his hands. He could direct the car like he did a baseball, with his arms and hands. He wasn't afraid of what he was doing.

He turned at the big fairground sign and went through the gate that was open for the drivers. He idled the car for a moment, looking out at the track and the empty infield. In his mind he could hear the noise of the race. He could see the trailers and pickups in the infield. He could hear the sputtering microphone and the revving of engines. He could see Casey in the stands. He could see Gwen, too, and Taylor in his Mercury next to this fat white Chrysler that could most likely outrun everything in sight.

He pulled out on the track; he could see it differently now. The track had been washed down that morning. There was a sticky-looking surface on the packed, dry dirt. He could see the chugholes, the dilapidated fence, the curve that made the backstretch seem to disappear. He started slowly, feeling the dirt under the wheels. It was a new sensation, this churning dirt around him. Yet he remembered it, too—the dust choking him as his body churned into home plate.

He gave the Chrysler more gas and shifted into second. The car jumped with his uneven clutching and he remembered how his leg lifted and turned in one even, continuous motion when he threw a good pitch. On the next shift, the car responded perfectly. He could drive. He felt it in his hands and feet. His stomach heaved and he let go of the wheel for a second to shake his hands in the air. He could drive!

The track was getting familiar to him. He could take the first curve in second. With all that room out there and no other cars crowding him, he could take it in third. He could drive without shifting at all.

Casey saw the dust rising from the track before they got there. "Look!" she said to Taylor and Gwen in the front seat.

"I thought they were going to water that track down

this morning. It's gonna be like driving in a quarry," Taylor said, turning into the gate.

"It's a car," Casey said. "Taylor, somebody's driving out there."

"Oh, damn." Taylor pulled up near the track and got out. "Somebody's chewing the damn thing up!"

Casey was watching the car. She had seen it somewhere before but couldn't remember where. She just knew her association with it wasn't a good one. The car pulled out of the last corner and offered them a sideways view of itself in the dust. "Taylor, that's Dwayne!"

"You're kidding!" Taylor squinted at the backside of the Chrysler as it skidded through the first turn. "Good grief, I think that's Alva Pickens's car!"

"It is, and that's Dwayne driving it. I know it is!"

"Why, that man's crazy as a loon," Gwen said from between them.

"You've got to stop him, Taylor," Casey begged.

"How? Just tell me how? Walk out there and get smashed to smithereens?" Taylor gave his own car an angry, frustrated fist.

"He's gonna kill himself," Gwen said. "We're gonna stand right here and watch that ignoramus kill himself."

"Taylor, we've got to stop him!" Casey screamed. She put her fists over her eyes so she couldn't see him pass.

"I can't think," Taylor said, on the verge of tears himself. "Dammit, I can't think of any way to stop him, Casey."

"He sure is tearing the devil outa that track," Gwen said. "If this was a race he'd either win or die trying."

"That's it! That's it!" Casey was racing toward the

announcer's stand. "Taylor, how do you turn this thing on?"

Taylor raced up the steps behind her. "God help us, this had better work, because if it doesn't we'll have to wait until he gives outa gas or goes over the side." He flipped on switches and they heard the static of the speakers.

Casey picked up the mike and pressed it against her mouth. Her breath whistled out across the field. "Ladies and gentlemen! This has been a sight to see! Here on our famous track, the great driver Dwayne Pickens has just shown us a display of his skill and daring at the wheel of a white Chrysler, making better time than has ever been run here, even by that all-time favorite Taylor Flanagan!" She paused to get her breath while the car continued its careening laps below. "Ladies and gentlemen, Dwayne Pickens has won the race!" she shouted into the mike. "Dwayne Pickens is the winner! Dwayne Pickens, please bring your car in and accept the trophy!"

In the distance they could hear a police siren.

"Jeez," Gwen said. "What's the fuzz doing out here?"

"Dwayne does not own a car," Taylor said, his voice cold with frustration as he watched the track.

"Will the winner, Dwayne Pickens, please bring his car in!"

Dwayne could hear his name. At first, it was like the voice speaking those familiar sounds was coming out of the car itself, but then the rhythm changed and the sounds took on a frantic tone. He tried to peer through the dust to his right, but he couldn't see except straight in front of him. Still he heard his name. It was coming from the loudspeaker! He slowed down a little and rolled open his window. He had won! That was what they were saying. Dwayne Pickens had won the race! He should come get his trophy, the voice was saying. He pressed the brake and the car, caught at such speed, screeched, skidded and settled facing the spectators' stand. Dwayne crawled out of the window like Taylor always did and stood looking up through the dust at the announcer's stand.

He could see a police car coming, its siren whirring, and then Alva's second car behind it. Still he watched the announcer's stand, waiting for the appearance of his trophy. It was Casey who came down.

"Did you see me win?" he yelled to her. "I won! Did you see?" He bounced up and down beside the car. "I'm getting a trophy! Did you hear that!"

Taylor was getting something out of his car. It was a little silver-plated loving cup Gwen had given him to keep in the pocket of his Mercury. She had had *The Greatest* engraved on it.

"You can't give him that!" Gwen said, trying to pull Taylor back. "I gave you that. That was a present! Taylor Flanagan, if you give him that, you've seen the last of me!"

"Hush, Gwen," Taylor said. "And smile."

"The winner, setting a speed record unmatched on this track, is Dwayne Pickens!" Taylor shouted, setting the cup into Dwayne's waiting hand.

"Look at it, K.C.!" Dwayne said. "Look at it!" He thrust the cup at her.

"It's terriffic, Dwayne. It's the best trophy I've ever seen."

"What's going on here?" the policeman said to

Taylor, looking from one potential culprit to another.

"We had a little test run going here, George," Taylor said, moving away with him toward where Alva was examining his Chrysler.

"My brother stole this car," Alva sputtered. "He stole it and drove it out here without a license and practically tore it up racing around this track."

"Whose car is it? the officer wanted to know.

"Why, it's mine," Alva shouted. "You know it's mine."

"And you want to take action against your own brother?" the officer said. He was taking out his pad.

"No, he doesn't," Taylor said.

"You stay out of this, Taylor Flanagan. You're responsible for this anyway. Nobody else would teach a moron how to drive. It's you and these goddamn races. You ought to close this place down, Officer. Nothing but riffraff comes out here, anyway."

"I'm driving the second race this afternoon," the officer said to Taylor. "I guess you are, too."

"Yeah, if we can get the track back in shape."

"What about my car?" Alva asked, his indignation slightly dampened.

"Doesn't seem to be much damage to it," George said. "Any body shop can knock those little dents out in an hour. Get her washed up and maybe get her tires checked. This track is hell on tires."

"Officer," Alva said, trying to be calm. "My brother stole my car, this car, out of my garage with my wife standing right there, and he drove it without a license to this racetrack, where he proceeded to show himself for the moron that he is."

"George," Taylor said, turning his back to Alva. "It seems to me that whereas his wife saw him taking the car, he was more borrowing it than stealing. And whereas we didn't see him drive it out here, we can't say for sure that he did. And since the car isn't damaged, I don't see what the problem is."

"He's right about that, Mr. Pickens. Besides, everybody knows Dwayne."

"Then everybody should know he presented a danger to the public today," Alva said.

"To your car, maybe," George said. "But, so far, Dwayne has never, ever hurt a person, and he doesn't seem as likely to as the rest of us do. Now let's get your car outa here. I'll go by in a little bit and have a talk with your mama about this. We just got to make Dwayne understand he can't go around driving cars, that's all."

Taylor got into the Chrysler and drove it off the track. "There she is, Alva," he said. "We'll get somebody to drive it home for you in a little while."

"I'll do it right now," Gwen said. "I was leaving anyway, in case you'd forgotten, Mr. Flanagan." She slammed the door of the filthy car and drove it furiously through the gate and onto the highway.

"Gwen's kinda riled up," the officer said, slapping Taylor on the shoulder.

"Yeah, she's got a temper all right. Just one of the many charming things about her." Taylor grinned. "Listen, George, I'll keep Dwayne with me the rest of the afternoon. Casey here's a friend of his. They'll be all right. I'll see he gets home."

"That's right, Taylor," Alva said bitterly. "You take care of him. But you'd better decide if you are willing to do it every day, because if you're not, you better stay outa this. Somebody's got to be responsible for him.

Chapter Eleven

He ought to have been in training school or somewhere years ago, before he was so set in his ways, but
Mama and Daddy wouldn't have it. Now it's up to me,
and I'm not going to have him all over town making
a nuisance of himself."

"Just what does that mean, Alva? Sounds like out of
sight, out of mind to me," Taylor said.

"We'll see," Alva said, "although it's none of your
business what I do."

"Let's get outa here, Mr. Pickens," George cut in.
"Don't want you mixing with this here riffraff."

They pulled away, passing a line of pickups and cars
pulling trailers through the gate. Taylor turned to
Casey and Dwayne who were sitting on the bottom
row of the bleachers.

"You were great," he said. And each of them knew
just who he was talking to.

· 12 ·

*W*here *could she put* the pain? That was what Pansy Whitaker wanted to know after those first days when her grief stopped its spreading and she felt her body filled to the brim and leaking sorrow like tears. She knew she must contain it somehow, control the ache's relentless pursuit of her mind and spirit. She knew she couldn't suffer any longer, at least not so passionately, so willingly, for the pain had become too close to her, almost dear, like a companion she'd grown comfortable with.

At first, when feeling anything seemed such a blessing to her, she had welcomed the pain because she dreaded numbness, that undisputable sign of life's ebbing, most of all. In the beginning, she had reasoned that if Hazard Whitaker were not sharing her table and bed, then bereavement would.

But now she wanted to live, not mourn. Now she wanted the old, sustaining pattern of her days, the familiarity of her single life again. Yet the pain stayed and with it, its own little irritations. She didn't like the constant threat of tears or the wan, trembling face she saw in the mirror. She worried about meeting Hazard on the street, about meeting anybody for that matter. The only people she felt comfortable with were Dr. Kemble's patients. They were sick like her. They didn't know or care that her marriage had ended before it was begun. All they wanted was release from pain— and that was what she wanted, too.

Jane came to see her. Every evening between dusk and dark, she would leave Ben and Hazard on the porch and go down the sidewalk to sit with Pansy on her porch. The two men were always silent. So were the women, but it wasn't a natural kind of silence, not the comfortable silence between people who knew each other well enough not to need conversation. No, it was a looming silence; it was like a third person who kept them from speaking their minds sat between them.

Still, Jane came because she loved Pansy and because she refused to let Hazard come between them now, just as she'd refused to let Ben affect their friendship years ago. What she felt for Pansy was worth keeping, was worth this silence that pushed itself between them.

"I know I must go on living," Pansy said finally, and the silence she broke shattered around them like tiny shards of glass they must be careful not to tread on.

Jane waited, avoiding the glass.

"I know I must put the past behind me," Pansy continued. "But where do I put the pain? I don't know what to do with a hurt that can't be cured. There's no remedy, Jane. I've faced that."

Still Jane waited.

"Twenty-five, even ten years ago, Hazard and I could have been happy together, but now it's as I've always feared it would be. As the years slipped by, I knew it was going to be too late for us. I knew we'd missed our chance for happiness. Hazard knew it, too. We both knew, and yet we let ourselves be hopeful. Now I know we were foolish. So foolish."

"That's what Hazard is saying, too," Jane said. She rocked her chair gently and it creaked on the porch floorboards. "That's what both of you are saying—how it was doomed from the beginning. How you're too old, too set in your ways, too hurt. But, Pansy, I've been thinking about this situation for two weeks now, since that morning when Hazard showed up hangdog on the back porch with you down here in your house alone like you'd never intended to be again. I've been thinking ever since that morning that you and Hazard, both of you, are too lazy. That's what it is. Laziness. Sure I know you've got to feel pain for whatever happened in Washington. So does Hazard. But after that, you've got to stop making excuses for this mess and start doing something about it."

"I can't," Pansy wailed. "Don't you see? I can't speak to him. I can't even stand to think about him. You don't know what he did to me, Jane. You don't know!"

"No, I don't. But I know this. Whatever Hazard did, it wasn't immoral and it wasn't against the law. That means it's something you can forgive. After all, he's your husband."

Pansy hadn't thought of him as that, not since that morning when she'd waited for him in their hotel room. She had handed him her wedding ring when she boarded the train for home. Wordlessly, she had dropped it into his open hand and then quickly put on her glove, covering her naked finger. She wasn't used to the ring anyway, and by the next day she didn't miss it at all. She put her mother's dinner ring back on her right hand, where she'd worn it for thirty years, and it felt comfortable and right. She liked the ring, although it was a bit gaudy with too many large stones and a heavy gold band. Pansy thought it said something about her father rather than her mother because he had selected it more, she knew, for show than for beauty or sentiment.

Hazard was like her father in that—always one for the gesture, making a show of things, but weak on relationships and commitments. She had taken good care of her father, but she hadn't always liked him. He had been demanding at times and inconsiderate, and for someone who had received an expensive university education, not very cultured. Everybody always thought he was cultured, though. Doctors were expected to be. But Pansy knew all that training didn't mean he knew anything about art or beauty or that he read anything beyond the front page of the paper.

Of course, what did that have to do with Hazard, who probably hadn't graduated from high school? She'd never asked him that. In all those years, she hadn't asked him anything about his education, assuming of course, until now, that he had one. Hazard seemed like the kind of man who had many opportunities—he was, at least, more than a little clever—but had never bothered to take them. Pansy both despised and admired his unwillingness to care much what people thought of him. She wished she didn't care that the whole town knew they'd come home from their honeymoon separated. Well, if she was the one who cared, then she should be the one to do something about it.

"Why, Jane, I think you're right," Pansy said suddenly. "What's needed here is some plan of action. I should either take Hazard back or else I should get an annulment."

"An annulment? Why, Pansy, of course you're going to take Hazard back! Of course you are. And I shouldn't be down here pushing you. You need time. A lot of time. Now I think you should at least see Hazard, talk to him. Why, you could come for supper tomorrow night like always. Do that, Pansy. See him."

"I'd be delighted," Pansy said.

CASEY WAS worried. The house seemed full of mourners —Hazard stuck in his room, avoiding her and Jane as if he were ashamed of something. Taylor was silent too, because Gwen turned her back on him at the candy counter when he tried to talk to her and didn't show up for last Saturday's race. Taylor lost. A new driver, a boy in his teens from a neighboring county, had shown up in a 1946 Ford that looked unbeatable, and was. Taylor barely managed to hold second place, but Casey could tell his mind wasn't on the race, anyway. He was missing Gwen a lot more than he'd thought he would.

Jane was always down at Pansy's trying to find out what had happened that put Hazard back in his old room and had left Pansy teary-eyed and humiliated. That left Casey with Dwayne, who seemed oblivious of the trouble he'd caused by taking Alva's car even after the officer had come and talked to him and his mama. Alva had come, too, with a lecture that Dwayne knew by heart.

"Hey boy," he said to Casey, who was sitting on the porch swing in the heat of the day, biding her grandmother's warning that summer sickness struck the over-heated more than other folks. She pushed the swing with her bare foot and sent it sailing. Dwayne sat down in a rocker and watched her.

"Hey Dwayne," Casey said. She leaned back and let the hot breeze wash over her neck and face.

"Whatcha doin', boy?" Dwayne asked. He pounded the arms of the chair restlessly.

"Nothing. It's too hot to do anything," Casey said.

"We could ride my bike," Dwayne suggested.

"Too hot."

"We could go to the picture show."

"No money. Besides, we saw it yesterday."

"Go swimming."

"Uh-uh." Casey had a swift vision of herself in her two-piece swimsuit and almost laughed out loud. "How come you don't like girls, Dwayne?" she asked.

"Oh, they ain't worth nothin'," Dwayne said, ducking his head. He stopped rocking. "They make me feel bad, that's all it is," he said after a while. "I starts to thinking how they look so pretty sometimes, but then I remember how they can't do nothin'. Can't play ball, can't run worth nothin'. All the time combing their hair and wearing them frilly clothes, afraid of a little dirty spot on 'em. They just ain't fun, that's all."

"But you like Gwen and my grandma and your mama."

"They're different," Dwayne said. "Why, Gwen, she's Taylor's girl friend, and your grandma, she's been good to me ever since I can remember. And Mama, shoot, she's my mama. Anyhow, ain't none of them girls."

"Let's play cards," Casey suggested. "I've got some

animal rummy cards in the house. We can play until it cools off a little and then we can ride your bike."

Dwayne drew and matched his cards carefully, like he'd seen men do playing poker in the movies. Casey watched him play, his bent-forward concentration as he studied the silly animals. He was so involved in the game, so absorbed. Casey knew that his concentration on whatever he was doing accounted for so much of his trouble—it meant somebody else had to be watching out for him, protecting him from the world he didn't seem to know existed. Like his not understanding about the war in Korea. But then, who did understand it? What if he forgot it was even going on and asked her, like he sometimes did, "Where's your daddy, boy?" When she told him, he seemed to understand better than other people, even if he had to be told again and again. He took what he understood personally.

The world he knew was so very close to him. The houses and streets and people he saw every day. The food his mama cooked and the popcorn and sweets he bought at the picture show. The tobacco he chewed. His own moving body, and the announcer's voice on the radio that brought Crosley Field and Yankee Stadium into his head so that he could see the plays as clear as day. The determination that let him take Alva's car and the pleasure Taylor's little trophy brought him. Dwayne understood it was better to win, even when the game was animal rummy.

So she let him. Sometimes he won outright, and a couple of games Casey won fair and square, but mostly she arranged his victories. She liked to watch his slow grin forming long before he knew it was there, when he saw he had a chance to beat her. She liked the way he slapped the final pairs onto the porch floor and rolled his head back with glee.

"Hey boy, I got you good. See, I got you."

He could keep playing all day as long as he was winning. But he wouldn't always win. Already Casey had heard that Alva was talking about sending him away again. She'd heard all the arguments—how he needed to be trained in a menial skill, how he needed to understand discipline, how he was too old to be playing baseball with an oil drum, how his mama wouldn't always be there to take care of him. The talk hadn't reached Dwayne yet—it was as far away as Korea—but Jane and Ben Flanagan had heard it, so Casey knew it was true. She couldn't really imagine what such a place was like, but she knew Dwayne didn't want to go there and that was all that mattered to her.

"Let's go downtown," she said suddenly, dropping her cards on the floor. She didn't care about any dumb polio. She just wanted to get away. She wanted to feel free, to leave the cares that plagued her house and run away from the summer's silent, endless lethargy. And she wanted to take Dwayne Pickens with her.

HAZARD WHITAKER brought his face dripping from the basin and up straight in front of the mirror into which he peered anxiously, as if he hoped to see another face there. He looked terrible. He knew that, even without Casey announcing it to him as she had that morning when she paused in the open bathroom door to watch him shave. Both of them had looked at his mournful drawn face, one side lathered like a clown and the other smooth and pink but sad.

His jaws hung down like a basset hound's. That's what Casey said, and she was serious about it, too. He had a good face, but it was a face that needed to smile, especially with the jowls of his middle years hanging on no matter how many chin-ups he did. His eyes were baggy, too, and he needed a haircut. Gray sprigs stuck out around his ears—ears that seemed to be getting bigger and were sliding down his head, soon to be located on his wrinkling neck. A basset hound—that was what he looked like. No wonder Pansy wouldn't have him.

He dried his face and neck and turned away from the mirror without looking again. He didn't want to face the truth, although it seemed to be bumping into him every time his mind starting turning over his problem with Pansy. He knew she hadn't minded the way he looked. She'd seen his aging, just as he'd seen hers. He could remember her perfectly from years ago when she was perfect, but that didn't mean he didn't like the way she looked now. He could think how she looked twenty-five years ago beside how she looked on their wedding day and he'd take the wedding-day look, fine-powdered wrinkles and all. So why hadn't he taken her?

Opportunity had knocked at his door, handed him the finest prize a man could ask for, and he'd wasted it in a hotel bar with a couple of cronies he'd had to introduce himself to because they'd forotten him. Damn! Ten years at least he'd ridden the train with those guys, and they didn't know him from Adam until he told them who he was and what he'd been selling. That's what identified him on the road—his product. Well, he didn't have a product anymore. No product, nothing to sell but himself, and he'd made one hell of a mess outa that.

He went back into his room and put on a clean shirt. He knew the rest of the family was waiting for him. Casey had gone down five minutes ago and he'd heard Taylor's car in the drive. Somebody was playing the record player. Jane and her Frankie Carle records. They were all she ever bought, but they sure beat that stuff kids were playing nowadays. "Mockin' Bird Hill" and Nat King Cole singing "Too Young." Hazard started humming involuntarily.

"They say that love's a word ... A word we've only heard ... And don't begin to know the meaning of ..."

Damnation, once that thing got into your head, it was there for good. Hazard tied his tie, still singing softly to himself. *"We were not too young at all."* No, we were too damn old, he thought, practically strangling himself with his knot.

He shut his door and started down the stairs. Before he reached the bottom, he heard her voice, softer than the others, but tuned to his ear like a whistle an animal hears. Stuck on the steps, he thought quickly of the modes of escape available to him. He could go back to his room and feign a stomachache. He could go out the window and across the roof to the kitchen, where he could shimmy down the porch post. He could race down the stairs and out the front door and not stop running till he reached Cincinnati. Or he could face the music.

He could continue down the stairs and into the dining room where he could sit next to Pansy like always with everyone pretending nothing was wrong. Surely that was what Pansy intended to do. She must want to do that. Why else would she be here when she knew he was here, too? Obviously, she didn't intend to let one mistake ruin their lives. Well, neither did he. Besides, he missed her. No matter how angry she was, no matter what kind of icy look she intended to give him, no matter how she planned to ignore him, he wanted to look at her. He knew when he looked at her, he would believe again that loving her wasn't wrong. He didn't want it to be wrong. Loving Pansy was the most right thing he'd ever done, even if he'd botched it up and lost her for a while.

He went into the living room. Through the open door into the dining room he could see her, much as she'd viewed him in that Washington bar. She was smiling, her hand covering Jane's on the table. She was at home and comfortable. Her face was serene, clear of the pain he'd seen in the train station. Everything was all right! Praise God, it's all right! he thought, and bounded into his place before he could stop himself.

The food moved carefully around the table. Casey, across from him, looked from Hazard to Pansy and back, searching for some clue to the mystery of their dilemma. Ben and Taylor concentrated on eating. Jane gave her attention to Pansy as if she felt she could deter a confrontation by talking about the weather.

Hazard pushed his food around his plate. From the corner of his eye, he could see Pansy's hand on the table, her fingertips touching her water goblet. Her hand was perfectly shaped, so delicately curved, so bare. He wanted to put his hand over hers. He wanted to slip the wedding ring in his pocket back on to her finger and press his mouth to it.

She seemed to know what he wanted because her hand went swiftly to her lap, and she spoke, looking at Jane, but as if she were making a speech to all of them. "I saw a lawyer today."

It was what he'd feared most, and fearing it so, had made it the one possibility he could not consider. Hearing her words he knew there would be no reconciliation, no gradual renewal of their vows, no wooing. It would all be over unless he could stop her.

"But Pansy—" Jane started and then, seeing Hazard's face, fell silent. This is for him to do, she thought, and stared at her plate.

"I won't give you a divorce," Hazard said.

"You don't have to. I can get an annulment." Pansy still wasn't looking at him.

Her not looking at him stung worse than what she was saying. He wanted to see her eyes springing with tears. He wanted to see her quivering mouth.

"Look at me," he said. "Pansy Whitaker, you look at me."

To his surprise, she did. She turned sideways in her chair to face him. Clear-eyed, firm-jawed, without a hint of remorse, she stared him full in the face.

"You could have told me," Hazard began, more panicked than ever. "You didn't have to go racing off to a lawyer the first thing!"

"The first thing!" Pansy shouted. "The first thing! Two weeks, Hazard Whitaker. Two weeks since that fiasco in Washington! Two weeks and that's enough! No more feeling sorry for myself. No more moping around like I've lost my best friend, which, thank God, I have not! Jane said I needed to take action and I agree with her—"

"But I meant—" Jane started.

"I know, Jane, I know," Pansy said. "But you can't change him, I can't change him. I never could. I never even wanted to. I thought I could love him just the way he was." She turned back to Hazard. "But I can't."

He was the one who was going to cry. He looked at Casey, who was fiddling with her fork and pretending she was deaf. He wished she'd look at him. Maybe her face, her youth, would tide him over, but she couldn't lift her eyes any more than he could stop the tears that rolled down his cheeks.

"Don't," Pansy said in a normal voice. "Don't let this hurt you, Hazard."

"But it does." Hazard wiped his eyes with his napkin. "It was terrible what I did," he said to the table at large. "I know that. I mean, first I didn't reserve a berth and there we were, sitting up all night on the train. And then Pansy left her bag in the station and I was waiting for it in the lobby when I saw these two fellas from the old days and we had a couple of drinks and time just went away. Everything left me. Everything. Even you, Pansy. I admit that. I forgot about you up there in that hotel room waiting for me. I'm sorry for that. More sorry than I've ever been for anything I've ever done."

"You mean nothing happened?" Casey howled.

"Casey!" Jane slapped the table and the dishes rattled.

"Nothing happened," Pansy echoed. "And there's no changing that either. And because nothing happened,

I can get an annulment and have my old name back and my old house and my old life." She was sniffing.

"Then I'll just have to try to stop you," Hazard said, "because you're talking about my life, too, and I don't want my old life back. You want action, huh? Well, you'll see action!" He grabbed her hand out of her lap. "You see this?" He yelled. "I'm gonna put a wedding ring on that hand if it's the last thing I ever do!"

"And it will be!" Pansy said, wrenching her hand free. She pushed away from the table.

"Where are you going?" Hazard asked.

"Home." Pansy stood as straight and prim as she could.

"I'll walk you," Hazard said.

"No, thank you."

"Then I'll walk behind you." Hazard stood up, too.

"Hazard, please."

"Please what?"

"Please leave me alone."

"I can't. I love you and I've left you alone too damn long as it is."

"Jane—Ben." Pansy looked helplessly around the table.

Everybody ignored her.

"Casey—" Pansy was backing through the kitchen door with Hazard going toward her.

They heard the kitchen door slam and sat, their faces hot and their mouths struck with foolish smiles, while Casey raised her fists above her head and shook a Dwayne Pickens victory salute. "Nothing happened!" she crooned. "Nothing happened!"

· *13* ·

The first weekend in August it rained. Late Friday, before the sun had time to fade into dusk, dark clouds swept in on a high wind and massed in dark patches on the surface of the sky. Jane Flanagan brought the geraniums in from the railing and leaned the porch chairs against the wall of the house. Dwayne Pickens scooped up his bag bases and slug them in his garage beside his bike, then yelled good night to Casey, who sat on the porch swing watching the moving clouds and waiting on the first hard crack of lightning that would send her scurrying into the house.

Taylor went to bed right after supper when the rain was just beginning to gust against the closed windows of his stuffy room. He lay there for a long time thinking about the race the next day, imagining how the track would be choked in mud, hiding new chugholes and spraying his windshield with a thick layer of mire.

He was thinking about Gwen, too. He couldn't seem to think about anything—not racing, not weekends, not even getting through his day—without thinking about her. He'd have his mind on the race and a spot of white light would catch his eye and he'd think it was Gwen, swinging that blond ponytail in the stands. But it wasn't. Hadn't been her for three Saturdays since he gave that stupid tin cup to Dwayne Pickens. Well, he'd get another cup, he'd get ten cups. But she wouldn't listen to him. She'd turned her back on him in the five and dime twice already, one time to wait on somebody, but the other time she was purely rejecting him. Showing she didn't care. Proving she didn't have a lick of feelings for Dwayne Pickins. He'd always suspected as much. But then, why should she?

Gwen hadn't been brought up with Dwayne. She hadn't seen him all those years struggling to fill up his days with something while everybody else grew up and had their days filled for them. She hadn't seen him when Alva took him away that time, like a convict or something, although Dwayne had been willing to go. And glad to come back. He'd told everybody in town, like they were as happy as he was. "I'm back!" he yelled to everybody in sight. "See, I'm back!" Like anybody cared.

The stuffy room had put a sweat on him. Taylor got up to open his door but then lay down again. He could hear Casey singing in her room, bored he reckoned, although she certainly never complained. This couldn't be the greatest summer the kid had ever had, not with her daddy on her mind and the only word from her mother a telephone call every Sunday morning. Casey always just said yes and no, or the shortest answer she could think of, into the phone. It was sad, her not talking to her mother any more than that. Taylor didn't blame it on Barbara, though. She was doing the best she could. They all were. After all, this was a war, a little one by some standards, but a war nonetheless. People were getting killed in it. People were getting worked up over it too, what with General MacArthur going around making speeches and worrying everybody about President Truman firing him just like people could get him his job back. Why the devil anybody would want that job was more than Taylor could understand. He didn't see why anybody would want to be president or a general or even a pilot. And if it didn't make sense to him, how could anybody expect Casey to understand it?

One letter she'd had from David. One lousy letter in two months. Well, what could he say? "Killed twenty Commies today. Wish you were here." or "Bailed out this morning. In hospital. Daddy is a gimp." At least the letter she got was a real letter. Two pages in David's tight, clear script. He didn't talk about the war at all, but about how he hoped she was O.K. and how he wanted her to be a good girl and how he remembered her and missed her. David could say things like that in a letter. His brain could pour out words his mouth would never say.

Taylor was like that himself. He couldn't imagine telling Gwen he loved her. If he did. Now there it was, the whole ball of wax. He couldn't even tell himself he loved her. He moaned into his pillow, kicked the sheet onto the floor, lay flat for a moment contemplating staying wide-awake for half the night, then got up and went across the hall to Casey's room.

She was reading, the book propped on her knees very close to her face. The lamplight shining on the page and the side of her face made her look spooky against the white sheet.

"Hi," Taylor said, thinking how much like David she was when she was quiet like this. He remembered

David reading with a flashlight, that eerie glow diffused on the bed and floor where he huddled with a book long after bedtime. Mama wouldn't have minded his reading, but there had been something fun about the secretiveness of those hours that made the adventures in the book more breathtaking. "Whatcha doing?"

"Nothing." Casey put the book down. She was glad Taylor had come. The night had begun so early because of the storm and she saw the hours stretching in front of her, a dismal, lonely time with the house so quiet and defenseless against the gusting rain outside.

"Still raining," Taylor said, peeping between her curtains.

"Yeah." She was thinking of her daddy and the lecture he liked to give her about the weather, explaining in long detail the formation of clouds, the wind currents, the peculiar combinations that resulted in hail and hurricanes and typhoons. He explained hopefully, as if he could make her never fear the elements, but always when lightning popped across the sky, she was frightened. The thunder always startled her by its closeness. Maybe that was why her daddy knew so much about weather—to keep himself from being afraid.

"Couldn't sleep," Taylor said, settling on the foot of the bed.

"Didn't try," Casey replied. "Grandma won't have the television on because of the lightning, so I thought I'd read."

"Good idea." Taylor picked up her book and read the jacket. He gathered it was some sort of romance, a book about teen-agers in love. "Any good?"

"It's O.K. Gwen gave it to me."

"She reads this stuff, huh?" Taylor flipped the pages as if he could discern the true contents in a second. He dropped the book back on the bed, defeated. "She won't talk to me, you know."

"She talks to Dwayne and me, though," Casey said encouragingly. "I think that's a good sign. I mean, she's not mad with all of us. In fact, I think she's getting to like us a little. She's always glad to see us."

"Even Dwayne?"

"Even Dwayne. Taylor, do you think Alva's still mad over the car?"

"Probably. What the hell, Casey, maybe I shouldn't have shown Dwayne how to drive, but there he was, as much a kid as any kid could be, and you could see how he was just aching to get behind the wheel." He picked up the book and dropped it again. "But maybe I shouldn't have done it."

"I heard Grandma say driving the car might be all Alva needs to try to send Dwayne to the hospital again," Casey said. "You don't think he will, do you?"

"Who's to know? Alva is a peculiar man, very big on his public image. He likes living in that big old homeplace, he likes being on committees and the town board. He's the sort of man who gets a kick out of his name on brass plates in public buildings. So here he is, saddled with Dwayne, and instead of enjoying him just the way he is, he thinks he's got to improve him or else hide him away."

"Is that what he was doing the last time?" Casey wanted to know. She felt a heavy, desperate clutch of fear that she knew wasn't associated with the storm. "Hiding him away?"

"Since there's no improving for Dwayne, I guess it was."

"And if he tries to put him away again?" Casey asked breathlessly.

"We'll try to stop him, I guess. We didn't the last time. That was before he moved across the street and we just weren't paying much attention to what was happening. Dwayne had sort of drifted out of our lives then."

"But now he's right here," Casey said hopefully.

"He sure is," Taylor said. "And I guess that makes him our responsibility. Somebody's got to look out for him, sort of like the way we're looking out for you this summer, not that you need much of that."

"Sometimes I do," Casey said softly.

"Homesick, huh?" Taylor put his hand on hers.

"A little. Sometimes Mama seems as far away as Daddy is."

"That's natural. Two miles and two hundred can be the same when you're lonesome." Taylor was thinking of Gwen.

"You're gonna get her back," Casey said, grinning at him, "just like it happens in this book." She flipped the volume at him.

"Then I better read it, hadn't I?" Taylor laughed. Then he was solemn again. "I'll make you a bargain. You don't worry about Dwayne and I won't worry about Gwen. Now let's get some sleep."

"Taylor," Casey said when he had reached the door. "I'm glad I came."

She went to sleep with dreams that had no storms in them.

Down the hall, Hazard Whitaker was devising a plan. The scene with Pansy in the Flanagans' dining room that past Thursday had convinced him. He didn't care what he had to do, he would get that woman back. So he'd followed her home that night just like he'd told her he would. Walked five steps behind her because she didn't want him up front of her. Followed her right up the steps, onto the porch, and would have been in the house, but she was too quick for him and slammed the door before he saw for sure that she wasn't going to give way and let him in politely.

Twice this week he'd gone to Dr. Kemble's office to see her, had stood right in front of her desk lined with violets, his back to the patients who waited to be called, and said, "I didn't come to see the doctor, although I'm sick, Pansy, sick at heart, sick to dying in love with you. Aching, giddy, sick with love."

She'd tried to hush him up. She'd whispered and stammered the first time, taken unaware as she was. But the second time, she'd been ready. He'd seen the fire in her eyes the minute he walked in, closing the opaque-paned door behind him so the bell jingled merrily above their heads. He had started his speech anyway. If nothing else, maybe he could wear her down. But she came from behind her desk briskly and took him by the arm as she introduced him to the waiting patients one by one while Hazard continued his entreaties, spouting poems he'd memorized from ladies' magazines. She ignored his raving. "He's deranged, you see," she would say. "But we must be tolerant, don't you think? He's not at all well, but I'm certain he's harmless." Until Hazard was exhausted and escaped her fierce grip like he was the one being harassed.

Now he turned his mind to something serious, some proof that he wasn't so harmless. He would camp out in her yard. Already he'd discovered Taylor's pup tent in the garage, along with a few old pieces of Boy Scout equipment. If it wasn't too wet, he'd move tomorrow. Maybe even if it was still raining. Maybe she'd get his meaning if the lightning was still dancing in the sky when he staked the ratty old tent down.

They all overslept, the smooth sound of rain washing down the roof lulling them past seven o'clock. Downstairs Jane was frying bacon and Ben stood at the bottom of the stairs and called up to Taylor that they were running late. Taylor could envision the bright wet stacks of lumber, and he turned over into his pillow to avoid his daddy's voice. Casey also lay in bed, listening to the rain and wondering what she'd do with a rainy, miserable Saturday. If it cleared off enough, she could go to the racetrack that afternoon like she and Dwayne had planned; if it didn't, it was a wasted day. She pulled the sheet over her head and went back to sleep.

Hazard was up, thinking he was late. He wanted to get out there with his tent first thing. Maybe he'd wake her up pounding the stakes in and she'd come out on the porch wearing that robe he'd seen in her suitcase, barefooted, her face heavy with sleep, and she'd say, "Come in, Hazard," and he'd know she was caught in a dream but he'd come anyway to make her dreaming real. Once in her house, they'd both see that was where he belonged.

After breakfast, he collected his duffel bag, a knap-sack of supplies, and the little tent and went down the street to Pansy's. Her house was quiet, veiled in the soft morning rain. Above the rooftop there appeared a small slice of blue sky, as if the clouds were falling away from Pansy's house and their lives at the same time. He knew he was doing the right thing.

He lay the duffel bag on the front porch and went to work on the tent. The ties were stringy and brittle with age, but he pulled them as tightly as he could and swung the mallet against the metal stakes.

Pansy heard the sound, familiar yet close, in her sleep. Her eyes still closed, she thought she had dreamed the noise of Dwayne Pickens's baseball against the oil drum. But she was awake. She opened her eyes, still listening to the clang. It was too quick for baseball, too close, too definite. She got out of bed and slipped into her honeymoon robe, the peach silk she refused to discard even though the memories it held haunted her, and went to the window that looked out on the front yard. A dingy green tent was ob-structing her view of the street.

Dwayne, she thought immediately. Although why would he be in her yard when he had a yard of his own? Of all his childish antics, she'd never known him to invade someone's property like this. Of course, Casey could be with him, which would make it all right, al-though she would like to object to stake holes in her front yard. As a matter of fact, she objected to a tent in her front yard, no matter who was putting it up. She rapped on the window and stood aghast at the figure who rose from the other side of the tent. It was Hazard, his shirt sticking to his chest, his hair slick with rain. He grinned at her over the top of the tent.

"Come on out here!" he called as she dropped the curtain, backing herself deeper into the dark parlor, out of his light. "Come on out here, Pansy!"

She stood in the parlor, her hand at her throat. She had thought he was harmless. She truly had. She had thought she could get an annulment and when Papa Tutoni got well, Hazard would go back to being a waiter and show up occasionally at the Flanagans', but not too often that she'd have any problem avoiding him. She had thought he would let go. But now she knew he wouldn't.

She pulled the robe tightly across her breasts, her arm against her chest like a shield, and marched resolutely to the front door. "What are you doing?" she was saying before she even got out on the porch. "What do you think you're doing?" She had to get the offensive. She had to attack, else she was lost.

But Hazard had already invaded, had already claimed the ground she'd thought was sacred. Standing beside the shabby little pup tent and looking at that wide-eyed, sleep-brushed face, he knew if he persevered, if he were willing to weather this storm, he could get her back.

"Camping out," he said calmly. He didn't smile. A smile would give away his victory. He was going to sleep that night in a soggy tent. Maybe the next and the next. Maybe the rest of the summer, until the leaves made a soft dry bed around him and the ground grew the white crystals of early frost. Maybe till then. But someday she would give in. He could see it on her face, that expectant look she would try to deny, that bewildered needful expression that told him she wanted to be led by the hand back into the life they had begun. But not yet. He wouldn't press his advantage yet. Camped outside her fortress wall, he would starve her out, make her hungry for his touch and his voice until she would see that his winning would be her victory, too.

❧ *14* ❦

*T*he racetrack was in as
bad a condition as Taylor had expected.

"Maybe we ought not run," he said to the track
manager, who rolled his cigarette on his lip and looked
thoughtfully out at the muddy oval. He was thinking
about his money, how much he'd lose if these fools
didn't get out there and sling their butts around in that
mud puddle.

"Let's give it a try," he said finally, as if he'd been
thinking the situation over carefully. "Run one race
and then decide on the next. Got people on their way
out here, you know. Feel like I got to offer them something."

"'Yeah, well, I'll run if everybody else does," Taylor
said. He was watching the cars coming into the infield.
There were two unfamiliar ones. "Who's that?"

"Fellas from up in the foothills. Called me up last
week, wanting to come down here and run. Been running liquor up there for years and now they're thinking
to make some money legit."

"What makes you think this is legit?" Taylor wanted
to know. "You pocketing the cash and shelling out
those little trophies not worth the writing on them."

"You ain't gotta run, Taylor. Ain't nobody makin' you."

But Taylor had turned his back on the man and was looking for Casey and Dwayne. They were in the infield perched beside the Mercury on the trailer.

"Frankie, help us get the car off!" he yelled and clomped across the muddy track to his trailer.

The car was running good. Taylor had spent the last few nights in the lumberyard shack working on it. He loved the Mercury, but leaning over the fender, the light bouncing under the hood and his fingers slick with grease, he couldn't help but think about Gwen. He'd turned the radio on to that moody romantic music you could get late at night, and that little shack was the loneliest place in the world. But he knew Gwen wouldn't want to be there with him. He knew what interested her was the lumber business because she was always asking him about what they were selling and who bought it, about what the market was like. She didn't want to talk about cars. She wasn't interested in taking chances. Not Gwen. She was after a sure thing.

Now Taylor pressed the accelerator, listening for the clean smooth purr of his engine.

"It's O.K.," Casey said to him through the window. "Sounds good." She was wiping her hands on a grease rag like she knew what she was doing.

"You and Dwayne get on over to the stands," Taylor said, irritated with her. Why couldn't she act like a girl instead of turning into somebody he could rely on? Good grief, sometimes he got to thinking she was just trying to show Gwen up. Casey got involved in whatever was going on, she was willing to see the humor in things and make a good time out of nothing. Gwen just wanted to look good and strut around proud as a peacock. Well, he'd just about had it with her. If she wasn't here today, he was going to direct his attention elsewhere on a permanent basis, even if elsewhere turned out to be a carburetor.

He watched Casey and Dwayne sloshing through the mud to the stands. Out of the corner of his eye, he thought he saw a gleam of white there, but he refused to look. She hadn't come, wasn't coming, and that was that.

He slipped on his goggles and pulled his gloves tight against the tips of his fingers. The car grumbled under him as he eased out the clutch with a muddy boot. The other cars were pulling onto the track, too. Beside him was one of the new cars, its driver wearing a T-shirt and a cowboy hat. His gum rolled in his cheek before he spat it out the window and grinned at Taylor.

"How you do?" his mouth moved against the roar. Taylor nodded and looked back to the track.

They were playing the national anthem. Gwen was between Casey and Dwayne. She stood, her arms at her sides, face front but her eyes squinting toward the cars, hoping for a glimpse of Taylor.

She could see the car already rimmed with mud. He'll be filthy, she thought, and then stopped herself. She wasn't going to let that matter anymore. She wasn't going to care if he raced every Saturday for the rest of his life and gave every trophy he ever won to Dwayne Pickens. Not as long as he loved her.

The flag was down and wheels churned in the mud, trying to grip something solid. The spinning mire flew against the other cars, slapped windshields, and plopped into their sides. The good drivers moved on ahead, hoping their heat would begin to dry out the track. Nobody seemed to be really racing, just driving and trying to protect their cars. The laps moved slowly while the crowd twitched on the damp bleachers, bored with the lack of show.

Taylor was counting his laps and knew he was ahead. If he could win without damaging his car, that was O.K., too. Somebody had to get there first. But in the eighth lap, he felt someone moving in on him. It was one of the new cars, its sides thick with mud and its windshield wipers sliding over the splattered brown film on the glass. Taylor could feel the tension in the other engine, could hear the quickening power and the churn of intention the driver was putting into his anxious shifting. The new car couldn't be but one lap behind, not much under normal conditions but a lot when the track was bumper deep in mud.

Taylor could feel the car edging his backsides, and he started moving toward the fence to let the car pass. Give the kid a chance, he was thinking, although he knew he could get him in the backstretch where he knew the hidden holes like the back of his hand.

But the car wasn't trying to go around. Their bumpers touched and Taylor felt the heavy lunge of acceleration as the new car knocked into him. He's in a slide, Taylor thought, but he knew it wasn't so. The car had hit him intentionally.

He gave the Mercury gas and moved forward a little to give the car room to come around him. They were heading out of the first corner when the new car hit the gas and then slid into him broadside. It was no accident. Taylor looked across the car to his opponent.

He could see the glimmer of a smile under the dirty cowboy hat.

The new car moved on ahead of him, still a lap behind. Taylor slowed down a little, churning mud. He still didn't think the guy could win. But the new car was slowing down too, so they were abreast again, blocking the other cars when they took the last turn and came in front of the stands. Taylor saw the car moving in on him again, this time with unmistakable belligerence. He slammed into Taylor's side, the Mercury's mud-caked tires spun, lost traction altogether, and threw Taylor into the fence. He was out of the car in a minute, tearing off his goggles and gloves.

The new car was spinning its wheels, its slamming technique having momentarily crippled it. Taylor reached through the window and came out with a body struggling on his arm.

"It's a fight!" Dwayne was yelling from the stands. He dived over people, smashing hats and knocking cups to the ground as he headed for the track. The other cars were stopping behind the two front-runners and their drivers were crawling out.

The boy in the cowboy hat was dangling at arm's length from Taylor, grinning as if the prospect of a fight pleased him. He looked for his friend, who was coming around the cars behind Taylor, and then broke out of Taylor's grip to land a right under Taylor's jaw. Taylor slid against his car to get his balance in the mud and came out swinging.

"Where you goin'?" Dwayne said to the other new driver, who had broken through the circle of spectators. "Uh-uh! You stay right here." He shoved the wiry man against the car and turned to watch Taylor catching a blow in the stomach.

"Get 'em, Taylor!" Dwayne yelled. "Get 'em good!"

The man whom Dwayne had pressed against the car sprung to the side out of Dwayne's reach and headed for the action, but Dwayne went after him, catching him by the collar and spinning him around so that his fist could fit neatly under the fellow's chin. The man staggered backward and then slid down the side of the car, where his head settled heavily on his chest.

"Who's that?" Dwayne heard Gwen yelling from the sidelines. "Dwayne, see who that is!"

Two other strangers, obviously the mountain drivers' pit crew, were racing onto the track.

"Hey boy!" Dwayne yelled, catching one of them by the shoulder and decking him with a swing that would have meant a home run.

"Looka here, boy!" he said to the other one, pointing at the man he'd just decked. The startled opponent was still staring down at his companion when Dwayne landed him a right that sent him sprawling in the opposite direction.

"I'm gettin' 'em!" Dwayne yelled to his audience.

Taylor was still slugging it out with the cowboy, who came back grinning after every blow. The fight seemed to be what he'd been after all the time; Taylor, his head throbbing, one eye swelling fast, and his stomach still sucked in from the first hard blow, was tired of giving him what he wanted.

"Get in here, Dwayne," he yelled just as the mountain boy landed him a left that sent him down on his back in the mud. Looking up at the grinning face over him, he saw the sun behind his head darken for an instant and then heard the crack of bone as Dwayne let into the guy with his right. Blood sprang into the corner of the boy's mouth as he went down next to Taylor, dazed and oozing from the abrasions on his broken, bruised cheek.

"We got 'em!" Dwayne yelled. "Y'all see that? We got 'em!"

Taylor struggled to his feet and surveyed the damaged bodies in the mud. He was trying not to throw up. The smell of mud and heated engines was mixing with a burning stink in his throat.

"You all right, Taylor?" Casey was close to his face, a wet towel in her hand. She dabbed at his eye and cheek with the cloth and its rough texture grated on his raw skin.

"Yeah." He pushed the towel away to look through his one good eye as Gwen skipped across the muddy track, barefooted and holding her skirt out with one hand as if she were doing the minuet. "Taylor," she called. "Oh, Taylor."

"We got 'em," Dwayne said to her. "Cold-cocked 'em every one."

The mountain boys were coming around. George Greenwald flipped his badge out of his jeans in front of their teary eyes. "I could arrest you boys," he said, "but I ain't goin' to. Y'all too dirty to be messin' up the jail. But don't you come back here again. We all saw what you was doing."

"Picking a fight," Gwen said. She had Taylor by the hand and was leading him off the track. "Who you think you're messing with?" she asked the dazed faces. "This is Taylor Flanagan, that's who!"

"Y'all get on outa here," the track manager was

yelling to them from the sidelines. "I got a business here. I got to get them cars outa there for the next race."

"I'll drive yours off," Casey said to Taylor.

"No, we've had enough driving for one day. Let Frankie do it."

"Come on and sit down a minute," Gwen said. She was trying to direct Taylor without touching any of the places he hurt. "You poor thing."

The other drivers were backing off the track, spinning mud and laughing to each other. The fight had made them feel good.

"Who won?" Dwayne asked Casey as they went into the wet grass of the infield. Across the track, Casey could see Gwen and Taylor huddled together on the bottom row of the bleachers. He had his muddy arms around her.

"Nobody," she said, nodding in Taylor's direction, "unless maybe they did."

"I mean the race," Dwayne said trying to ignore the fact that Taylor and Gwen were kissing right in front of him. "Oh, shoot," he said, ducking his head. "*Yuk!*"

"Don't you think it's nice, Taylor and Gwen getting back together like that?" Casey asked, following him toward where Frankie was driving the Mercury up the ramp onto the trailer.

"*Pu-wee!*" Dwayne said, holding his nose and fanning the air with his baseball cap. "That love stuff makes me sick." He faked an upchuck into his hat.

Taylor and Gwen were coming up behind them, arm in arm.

"What's the matter with Dwayne?" Taylor mumbled, trying not to disturb his swollen face.

"Love makes him sick," Casey said.

"Well, you better get used to it, boy," Taylor said, gripping Gwen solidly around her shoulder, "because this here is a permanent arrangement."

Dwayne bent over to heave again, but this time it was for real. Peanuts floating in cola spewed over the trailer tire.

"He really is sick!" Casey said.

"Naw." Dwayne wiped his face with the towel Casey handed him. He gave them a half-sick, half-embarrassed smile. "I never hit nobody before, and it don't look like I take to it."

"Neither do I, Dwayne," Taylor said. He put his sore face against Gwen's. "Loving's got a lot more to it."

"Oh, shoot," Dwayne said, flailing the air with his cap again. But he was grinning at them. "Holy cow!"

"We can leave them here, making moon-eyes at each other," Casey said, "but that means we have to walk home."

"I want to ride," Dwayne said solemnly. "But, K.C., you got to get up there between them!"

"Not me," Casey said. "We'll just ride with our eyes shut. What we don't see won't hurt us."

"You two come on," Taylor said, pulling Gwen close to him. "I think we need to do some celebrating." He gave Gwen a long, breathtaking kiss.

"Holy cow!" Dwayne said. "There they go again!"

• 15 •

*T*he next morning, be-
fore the sun was more than a red streak above the
eastern woods, Taylor had stowed the rods and reels,
his tackle box, ice chest, and a worn bedspread in the
trunk of his car. Then he shoved a groggy Casey into
the back seat next to Dwayne, whose jaw worked anxiously as he struggled to abate his excitement. He knew
his whooping and hollering would wake up the whole
neighborhood.

He had never been to the ocean that he could remember, although his mama said he went once when
he was a little boy. She said he'd splashed right into
the waves like they were ripples in the bathtub and had
been sucked down and down until his daddy lifted him
out, sputtering salty water and sobs.

He had nearly drowned, his mama said as she put
his eggs in front of him this morning in her cluttered
kitchen. It was still dark outside, like night, and
Dwayne stirred catsup into the yellow scrambles and
tried to remember what the ocean looked like and how
it felt to be going down, down, where fishes tickled his
fingers and crabs slipped sideways toward his toes.

He couldn't remember. In pictures, the waves were

caught, blue and solid, heavy lips rimmed with white foam. They were like walls to walk into. He could not imagine them liquid.

"You're not to go into the water," his mama said. She was frowning as he looked at her over his eggs, the harsh kitchen light above her head like a hot white halo, and he sensed her foreboding, her memory of almost losing him once many years ago.

"I won't, Mama," he promised, forking the eggs into his mouth. "I'll stay with Taylor and K.C. We're going fishing anyhow."

So here they were, Casey dozing and Taylor humming while the car lights spotted just above the asphalt as the skylight turned slightly yellow, dawning a golden Sunday morning. They headed out of town to pick up Gwen. She was waiting, her bare arm on the cold metal mailbox, her shoes damp from having rested in the dew. She slid her bag behind the seat at Casey's feet and huddled up close to Taylor.

"I'm shivering," she said, wrapping one goose-bumped arm around his neck.

"Not for long." Taylor pulled back onto the highway. "It's gonna be hot out there. Hey, Casey, you bring a hat?"

"Yeah." Casey sat up blinking and looked around as if she couldn't remember getting into the car, much less the purpose of the trip. "A hat and a long-sleeve shirt," she yawned.

"Me, too," Dwayne said. He was glad Casey was waking up. "You ever been to the beach before?"

"Yeah, sure." She looked at him in time to see his grin begin to fade. He wanted her to be as excited as he was. He wanted this to be the first time for her, too. "A long time ago," she said. "I hardly remember it at all."

Dwayne grinned. "Me either. Mama says I near 'bout drowned."

"Well, we aren't doing any swimming," Taylor said, giving Casey a wink through the rear-view mirror. When he'd first thought about taking them to the beach they'd dealt with the dilemma of Casey's swimsuit by deciding to make it a fishing trip, although Gwen was wearing a suit under her shorts because she intended to soak up some sun.

"We could wade a little," Casey said.

"Long as I don't get my hair wet," Gwen said. "I want to eat someplace nice. Can't we eat somewhere nice, Taylor?"

"That depends on how nice you consider hotdogs to be."

She plopped a loud kiss on his bruised cheek. "Someplace nice, Taylor. Someplace with prime ribs and sour cream on the potatoes."

"At the beach? At the beach, you're supposed to eat seafood."

Gwen sighed and moved a little away from him. "I have something to tell you, Taylor."

Everybody straightened up to pay attention as if they expected an announcement that would affect them permanently.

"I can't stand seafood," she said.

The ocean stretched lazily before them as if it were just stirring from a night's rest.

"Tide's out," Taylor said, surveying the dark rippled strip of packed sand near the water's edge.

Chapter Fifteen

Dwayne leaned against the car, the rods and reels clutched in his hand like spears. A wave rose a little way out and spilled over into the surf. It was green water, dull for lack of sun because a patch of clouds midway the sky was holding back the sparkling morning light.

"It'll be O.K.," Taylor said. "We'll be grateful for a few clouds once that sun gets a chance at us. You'll roast out there." He passed Gwen the blanket. "The wind will get you even if the sun doesn't."

"I think I'll fish a little," Gwen said, frowning at the clouds. "As long as I don't have to eat them."

"Or bait them. Or take them off the hook," Taylor laughed.

Casey led the way into the pier shack, which turned out to be one large room haphazardly divided into bait shop, sundries store, and restaurant. The trapped rotten smell of dead fish mingled with the hot odors of chili and sizzling hamburger on the grill. The ice machine dripped its overflow of shaved ice through the floorboards and into the tiny waves that lapped against the posts below. Behind the bait counter were pinned pictures from newspapers and greasy photographs of fishermen holding up their catch. Below them was a blackboard on which were listed the hours of the tide and the weights of the season's record fish.

"One chili dog!" the cook shouted, slapping the paper wrapped sandwich on the counter. "Who wanted this here chili dog?"

"I'll take it," Dwayne called back.

"You order it?" the man asked, eyeing his unfamiliar customer.

"No, but I'll take it."

"Ain't givin' it away," the cook said, taking the hot-dog off the counter.

"You hungry already, Dwayne?" Taylor asked from the bait counter, where he was buying their pier permits. "Pin this to you." He handed them around.

Dwayne stuck the paper on his baseball cap and then put it proudly on his head. "Naw, ain't hungry. Just helpin' that fella out, seeing he cooked it and all."

"Where'll I put it?" Gwen wanted to know, looking down the front of her pink swimsuit. "I don't want pin holes ruining this elastic."

"Down there," Taylor said, eyeing her cleavage. "We can always get it when we want it."

"Aw, Taylor, you hush in front of these children." Gwen pushed the paper between her breasts. "I just hope it doesn't blow away."

"Not a chance." Taylor grinned and paid for a pound of shrimp the counterman brought dripping from cold storage. They followed him out the back door of the shack and onto the pier.

The weathered slats were like a track laid out in front of them and the pier seemed to drop down into the water at the end, following the curve of the horizon.

"Lordy, it's long!" Dwayne said, rubbing his head under his cap. He was still gripping the fishing equipment, as if he expected a sudden gust to blow both him and the rods away.

"Optical illusion," Taylor said. "We better go pretty far down, since it's low tide."

They followed him down the pier, Casey carrying the tackle box beside Dwayne, who kept looking down at the moving water between the boards.

"You'll be upchucking again," she warned. "Look out, not down."

Dwayne lifted his head to look at the expanse of ocean and sky surrounding them. "Who ever thought of so much water?" he said. "Who ever thought of so much everything? Look!" A gull was circling near them and they stopped to watch its sudden dip into the water.

"Having breakfast," Casey said.

"Don't you be getting my fish!" Dwayne yelled, shaking his fist at the gull, who was circling again. He laughed at his joke.

They were passing fishermen now, people who seemed asleep, their heads low against the ocean breeze, their permits fluttering on their clothes, necks and arms covered against the coming sun.

"Been out here all night?" Taylor said to one of them who seemed to be baiting his hook in his sleep.

"Since three. Nothing much," the man said, pinching off a bit of shrimp for his second hook. "Few spots. Expecting a run of croakers, though. Been expecting it two days now."

Near the end of the pier they found two empty benches side by side. Taylor divided the shrimp into a second container, put it between Dwayne and Casey, and then distributed the rods. "Three hooks to a leader, folks," he said. "I think the sinkers are about the right weight. When the tide starts in, we'll move up the pier a little."

Casey was already attaching her leader to the line. She slipped bits of shrimp onto the hooks. Fishing was something she felt comfortable with. Her father had taken her fishing, trusting her to maneuver the little outboard boat in the slow, brackish inlet water. They would spend the day moving slowly up the inlet, their lines dropping with no more than a single delicate splash, the only sound the deep chug of the outboard when they moved on and the steady click of their reels when they were still. They had caught pinfish, their chartreuse sides flicking between the dark water and the bucket in the bow of the boat. She could hear them flipping against the metal sides, shuddering life although their mouths bled and their gills fluttered. She had loved to fish as much because it was something they did together as for any other reason, although she liked the swell of moving water under the boat, the buoyancy that made her feel light herself, able to float, to swim, to dip deep below her world and lift out a treasure from another time, a primeval beauty welcomed with a spontaneous gasp of delight and a father's praise.

Dwayne had stuck himself with a hook and bent over his finger to conceal from Casey the thin trickle of blood he pressed from his thumb. He didn't want anyone to know he'd made a mistake. He wanted to do everything right.

"Got her ready?" Taylor asked him, having already sent Gwen's line out.

Dwayne wiped his hand on his pants. "Yeah."

"Then I'll show you how to cast. First thing," he said, taking the rod and reel from Dwayne, "is to make sure nobody's behind you. Caught a woman's hat one time. Took it right off her head and into the water. Then you do like this."

Taylor swung the rod over his shoulder with both hands, and the line spun off toward the water. "When the line's about down, start slowing it with your thumb." He let his finger lay gently against the spinning reel. "When it's down, you put the brake on until she's ready to reel in. Got it?"

"Yeah." Dwayne followed the steps carefully, an embarrassed smile edging his mouth. It was hard for him to learn things, he knew that. It took him a long time, and people didn't like to wait. Figuring on three hooks and this fancy business to let out and reel in made him nervous. He felt clammy with the damp wind blowing under his shirt. His thumb burned. He knew about fishing with a pole and some worms. Weren't nothing to it. Didn't catch much either, at least not in the creek outside of town, which was the only place his mama would let him go. Now this here was real fishing. This was serious business, and he intended to catch something at it.

The hooks and sinker sailed over his head and into the dark water below.

"Good cast, Dwayne!" Taylor said, grabbing his shoulder. "Atta boy!"

They settled down to fish while the sun moved slowly up, putting a sparkle on the water that now sent sloshing waves against the crusted pilings beneath them.

"I'm hungry," Gwen complained. She was holding the reel loosely in her hands, hardly paying any attention to the tension of the line. She seemed to be swaying with the pier, half asleep.

"I got something!" Dwayne yelled. His line was pulling away from him, straining in a slight curve toward the water.

"Easy now, boy," Taylor said. "Start reeling her in. Easy now. Don't jerk her."

The rod was dipping, too, pulling against the line that Dwayne slowly wound upward, out of the water. A croaker, its slick gray body glimmering with water and light, appeared above them as if by magic.

"A pound and a half if it's an ounce," Taylor said.

"I got one!" Dwayne yelled, holding out the fish still attached to the hook. "Looka here! I got one!"

"It's beautiful!" Casey said. "Here, I'll get him off. You go get ice to put him in."

"Naw, I'll take him off. You go get the ice." He put his hand out to catch the fish. The slippery body shivered in his hand. "You O.K., fish?" he said. He held up the croaker to a fisherman passing by. "See this one! It's a good one, ain't it?"

"Sure is, fella," the man said. "Best one I've seen all day."

"Hear that! It's the best one!"

Casey had arrived with the ice chest half full of shaved ice. "Get him off the hook and put him in here," she said.

"Naw. I wanta look at him."

"He'll rot," Casey said. "Just like that one." She pointed to a small shark left to shrivel on the boards. "He won't be good to eat."

"I'm not gonna eat him," Dwayne said. He got a tighter grip on the fish. "I'm gonna stuff him."

"Well, stuffed or not, he's got to go into the ice box," Taylor said. "Unless, of course, you want to throw him back."

"Uh-uh." Dwayne dislodged the hook from the fish's mouth and dropped him onto the ice. "That one's mine, though. You all know it's mine."

Chapter Fifteen

"I'm tired, Taylor," Gwen said. "I'm going on down and lie on the beach."

Casey felt a tug on her bait. "I think I've got something, Taylor," she said. "At least a nibble."

"Give it a few seconds. Too late and your bait's gone. Too early and you lose the fish, too."

Casey waited as long as she could and then started reeling in. They could see the silvery fish flipping and twirling on the hook halfway between the surface of water and the pier. Then the line was suddenly loose, the weight lost, and they saw the quick fall as the fish disappeared into the water.

"Lost him," Taylor said. "Too bad, Casey."

"He was a good one, though," Dwayne said. "Not as good as mine, but he was O.K."

"I'm going to eat a hotdog and drink a Pepsi and then go lie on the beach awhile," Gwen said. "You coming, Taylor?"

"Nope, I'll stay up here for now. You want to go with Gwen, Casey?"

"Yeah, I guess I will. Dwayne's having all the luck anyway."

They bought hotdogs and icy drinks in paper cups and took them down to the beach where they spread out Jane Flanagan's discarded blanket and sat down facing the water.

"So you're back together again," Casey said, having stuffed the hotdog into her mouth and washed it down with half the Pepsi.

"Thank God," Gwen said. She nibbled at the hotdog bun. "I was so lonesome, Casey. I didn't think I could get that lonesome. I mean, I always had a lot of friends.

I know a lot of people and all. I always had something to do, you know. But when Taylor and I weren't together, I just didn't want to do all that stuff. I just wanted him to come back. Of course, I knew he wouldn't. That day out at the racetrack I was so mad I just couldn't think how much I cared about him, but I wasn't halfway to town, driving that big old Chrysler, when I knew Taylor was right about doing something for Dwayne. I knew he was a better person than I am. I mean, he cares more than I do about people, but he's quiet about it.

"There I was in that big old car that rode so easy, like I was sitting on a pile of cushions and just floating along. But it was scary, too, like it could make me so comfortable I wouldn't notice how it was taking me away from what I wanted most in the world, until it was too late. I almost waited too late, didn't I, Casey?"

"I don't think so," Casey said, drawing a design in the sand with her finger. She put a stem on her flower, and tiny leaves. "Taylor was moping around there, him and Hazard, like they didn't have a thing to smile about. Couldn't get a laugh outa them for anything."

"He'd never tell me that," Gwen said. She held up her hand to shade her eyes. She could see Taylor and Dwayne on the pier. They were on the same bench, leaning against it more than sitting. She could see the points of their rods over the side and the bright yellow of Taylor's shirt. "He'll never say he missed me or that it was hard on him, too."

"Anyhow, he sure is smiling now," Casey said.

"Yeah, well," Gwen sighed and rolled over on her stomach. "He's got reason." She stretched her arm out off the blanket and let the sand fall between her fingers.

"One thing I've learned, Casey," she said, her voice muffled by the blanket and her drowsiness. "Don't ever make a person you care about have to choose between you and something else. Not if you can help it. Don't ever use yourself to bargain with. You ought to put a higher price on yourself than that."

Casey was still watching the pier. She could see Dwayne shaking his fist in the air, celebration for the fish that dangled at the end of his line. She knew not telling Dwayne she was a girl kept him from having to choose. She'd performed an act of kindness. That was what she'd thought. That was what she wanted it to be. But was it? Shouldn't she have taken the risk then, before they mattered so much to each other?

She lay back on the blanket beside Gwen. Through her shirt she could see the soft rise of her breasts. By next year this time she would be grown up, unable to hide beneath jeans and boys' shirts, unable to pretend. But not now, she thought, relaxing under the noon heat, her eyes shut against the brilliant sky. Right now I have this one last summer.

WHEN SHE woke up, Dwayne was sitting on the blanket beside her. He had pushed his bare foot deep into the sand and was packing more sand around it to make a cave.

"That's a frog house," Casey said, sitting up beside him. "A house for toads or toes." She rubbed her hands through her damp, matted hair, freeing it to the breeze.

Dwayne pulled his foot out carefully and then watched the mound cave into the hole. "Hell."

"I'll get some water," Casey said, picking up her empty Pepsi cup. "If we wet the sand a little, it'll pack better."

"I don't want to," Dwayne said, smashing the mound flat with his foot. "Four fish," he said. "That's all. And then Taylor says to me, 'Me and Gwen are walking down the beach a little ways. You go down there and stay with K.C.' And you sleeping. You come to the ocean and you sleep. Hell."

"You ought to quit saying that, Dwayne." Casey dropped the cup and grabbed his hand. "We'll go walking down the beach, too, and look for shells. Maybe we can even find a perfect sand dollar or some angel wings."

He didn't budge so she let go his hand and sat down again.

"Whatcha doing?" he asked her.

"Rolling up my pants legs. I'm going in the water."

"Mama said I couldn't." Dwayne dug his foot into the sand again, refusing to look at her.

"She said you couldn't go swimming. She didn't say a word about wading. There." Casey stood up and wiped her hands on her pants. "I'm going wading and shell hunting whether you go or not. But I wish you'd come. What's the matter with you, anyway?"

"Four fish," Dwayne muttered. He picked up the paper cup and stared into it. "Half a day fishing and four fish."

"I bet yours are the biggest, though," Casey said. "I bet you caught the biggest fish on that pier today."

"Bigger than Taylor's." Dwayne grinned. He was feeling better. Casey could always make him feel better.

Chapter Fifteen

"And now I bet we find the best shells on the beach. Which way do you want to go?"

Dwayne nodded toward the least congested end of the beach. He took off his shirt and Casey could see the white skin around the edges of his T-shirt, skin too pale to withstand the salty, burning wind, too delicate to contain such careless strength and childish grief.

She could not look, so she ran down to the water's edge, letting the surf wash over her feet and ankles, feeling the water pull the sand beneath her weight.

Dwayne followed her and splashed into the surf, his fishing failure pushed aside by this new adventure she was offering him. He felt the pull as the water swept back, washing sharp bits of shell around his white ankles. The water sucked at his feet and he remembered his mama's warning. He remembered the thick sandy water washing over his head, the close swollen pain in his chest, the briny water in his throat and nose. But now he was safe. His friend was there in the water beside him. There was no need to be afraid.

Beyond them the waves were lifting, subject to some hidden force, and then falling, lapping over each other as they churned inward, leaving spindrift in the air. A dusky afternoon glow lay over the water, and her hand above her eyes to shield them from the sun, Casey watched Dwayne spinning in the surf, knee deep in the warm foam, his arms flailing the wind like a wind-up toy. He seemed to collide with the air, a lone combatant of the elements. Then suddenly, as if he'd just remembered she was there, he turned to her, his face open, memory clear of all regret, and above the rush of falling water, she heard him call, "I love you, K.C. I love you best of all."

· 16 ·

*M*onday morning, Casey and Dwayne went down the street to inspect Hazard's new quarters. He was still there, squatting in front of a little Coleman burner over which an enamel cup of water was beginning to bubble.

"Making tea," he said, dipping a tea bag into the hot water. He looked bad. He hadn't washed in two days and his hair was sticking up in rebellious thatches all over his head.

"Grandma wants you to come down to the house and get cleaned up and eat a good breakfast," Casey said.

Dwayne was peering into the musty, sagging tent. "Holy cow," he said. "I wouldn't stay in there for nothin'."

"Neither would I. I'm staying in there for everything," Hazard said resolutely, swirling the tea bag in his cup.

"But you can eat, can't you? Grandma said what you did yesterday was your business, since it was Sunday. But this is Monday, a workday again, and there're certain things that have to be done."

"Like what?" Hazard blew on his tea.

"Liking eating, I guess, and shaving and—"

"Peeing," Dwayne added.

"Dwayne's right," Casey said. "The lilac bush may do in the dark of night, but this is daytime. Besides, you've got to go to work. Grandpa's expecting you this morning."

"She'll take the tent down," Hazard said. He looked gray, like a hobo sipping cheap wine over early morning ashes. "I know she will."

"She's gone to work, Hazard," Casey said. "Anyhow, I don't think she would do that."

"Yes, she would," Hazard said. "I'm an embarrassment to her. That's what she said to me yesterday. The only words she spoke in my direction all day was how I was an embarrassment and a disgrace."

"I had a tent once," Dwayne said. He had squatted next to Hazard and put his hands up to the fire although the morning was already warm and he had windburned streaks on his neck and arms. "Me and David and Taylor used to camp out in the front yard over on Plum Street. Sometimes at their house, too. It was a tent a lot like this." He turned suddenly to inspect the tent more carefully. "This is it!" he yelled, slapping the side happily. "This is it!"

"I hope you don't mind my borrowing it," Hazard said, looking even more dejected. No wife, no house, now no tent.

"You can have it," Dwayne said. "I wouldn't sleep in there for nothin'."

"Please go home, Hazard," Casey begged. "Just for a little while. Dwayne and I can watch the tent. You can even go on to work. Pansy won't come home until five o'clock like always."

"You'll watch it?" Hazard asked, looking from Casey to Dwayne and back again.

"We'll watch it, won't we, Dwayne?"

"Yeah, sure."

Hazard put out the stove and tossed the bitter tea into the flower bed. Then he trudged down the street toward a hot breakfast and bath, his every joint aching from the damp, cold ground and his mouth thick with remorse. Pansy had all the comfort. She had right on her side, too. She had everything.

He sat down on the back steps at the Flanagans', too weary to pull himself farther. She had won. Two days were all he could stand. Two days of potted meat and cheese. Two nights of wet, musty air too close to earth, too raw and solid for his old body. He put his hands over his face. He had lost her again, this time such a demoralizing defeat because he was simply too old, too full of pains, too tired.

"Hazard." It was Jane who lay her hand on his arm, reached around his trembling elbow, and pulled him up.

"There's breakfast on the table. Then I'll run you a bath and you can rest a while. Really sleep."

He heard sympathy in her voice. He heard her memory of their years together whisper in her gentle phrasing. He was the lost and found animal, the stray on her doorstep that she would love simply because he was there and needed her. Always before, he'd let her. Year in and year out, he'd willingly hung his head and nibbled at her generous hand. He'd rubbed himself against the Flanagans' warmth as if showing contentment would give him a permanent place there.

He lifted his eyes. "I'm going back," he said. "I have

to go back. My place is with Pansy now, no matter what I have to do."

"Today is not forever. It's just today," Jane said. "And if you don't win today, that doesn't mean you've lost. It just means you're holding your own. Some days that's all we can do."

"You think I'm foolish, don't you, Jane?" Hazard asked, letting himself be led to a chair at the kitchen table.

"No, Hazard, not foolish. I think you are brave, wonderfully brave. And if I were Pansy, I would love you very much."

DWAYNE WAS tired of watching the tent. After all, what was there to watch? At first, he inspected it carefully, crawling inside to look for David and Taylor's initials written with a crayon on the canvas. He found faint markings, but he couldn't read them. Then he crawled out and sat beside it, watching the flaps hanging loosely, and then the faded canvas that seemed to be smoking as the sun dried its moist surface.

"Let's go, K.C.," he said. "Let's go downtown."

"We told Hazard we'd watch the tent," Casey said. She was sitting on Pansy's step, out of the sun.

"But he ain't here so he won't know if we don't do it anymore," Dwayne argued.

"But what if Pansy comes home and takes it down?"

Dwayne's mind stumbled over that for a moment and then he brightened. "We could put it back up. Come on, K.C. Let's go."

"Well, for a little while," Casey said. She was bored, too, having long regretted promising Hazard their services. "When we get back, we can bring the gloves and ball over and catch some while we watch it."

They went downtown, having no mission but to confirm their freedom.

"There's the barbershop," Dwayne said, stopping to look through the window at the porcelain surfaces—black and white floor and counters gleaming like a photograph. "I get my hair cut in there." He waved at the barber, who waved back from beside a chair where he was bending over a man whose face was covered with a towel.

"Who's that?" Dwayne shouted through the glass. He pointed at the man in the chair.

The barber waved at them again.

"Who's that?" Dwayne shouted again, rapping his fingers on the glass.

The barber laughed and motioned them in.

"Hey boy," he said when Dwayne pushed through the door, pulling Casey reluctantly behind him. "Whatcha know, boy? Need a haircut?"

"Nope." Dwayne went right up beside the man still hidden under the steamy towel. "Who's that?" he wanted to know.

"Why, that's the mayor," the barber said, laughing. He was sharpening his razor on the strop. "Need a shave, Dwayne?"

Dwayne lifted the towel off the man's face so that a pinched, pink face emerged and blinked up at him.

"Don't look like a mayor to me," Dwayne said, dropping the towel back over the startled face. "Did he to you, K.C?" he wanted to know as Casey pulled him toward the door and out onto the sidewalk. She looked back to see the barber still sharpening his razor and grinning at them.

"Let's go see Gwen," Dwayne said.

They loitered along, looking in windows, catching their own reflections and grinning at their distorted sizes and foolish expressions.

"Look at that!" Casey said, stopping in front of a Schwinn bike in the hardware store window. "Just look at it, Dwayne!"

"You want that?" Dwayne asked, punching her lightly in the ribs. "You want that, boy? Well, hell, let's get it!"

"You don't have that kind of money, Dwayne," Casey said, pulling him away from the window. "Anyway, liking it doesn't mean I want it. Besides, I've got a bike at home."

They went into the five and dime, passed the magazines and school supplies, and right up to the counter where Gwen was scooping popcorn into long white paper bags and stacking them at one end of the warm popper.

"Hey," she said, smiling at them. "Want some popcorn?"

"No money," Casey said, pulling out her pockets.

"Me either." Dwayne grinned at her. He liked to see Gwen in her white jacket, looking so important and official.

"It's on me," Gwen said, handing a bag over the counter. "It's because yesterday was one of the nicest days I've ever had."

"Me, too," Casey said.

"Me, too," Dwayne echoed. "Except I didn't catch

enough fish. That much water, got to be a lot of fish down there." He shoved a handful of popcorn into his mouth.

"Next summer I bet we get a whole mess of fish," Gwen said.

"Hear that, boy?" Dwayne thrust the bag at Casey. "Next year we're going fishing again."

"Right now we got to get back to Hazard's tent," Casey said. "We got us a job watching it."

"What you all expecting it to do?" Gwen laughed.

"Nothin'." Dwayne frowned at her. "That's the whole trouble. It don't do nothin' and we don't do nothin'. Waste of a good day if you ask me. What we doin' it for, boy?"

"Because Hazard is afraid Pansy will come home and pull it down," Casey said.

"Shoot, it's about to fall down!" Dwayne hooted.

"Anyway, we got to go. Thanks for the popcorn," Casey said.

"You all have fun!" Gwen called after them.

"Ain't no fun watching a tent," Dwayne muttered as they went out to the street.

"Well, you don't have to," Casey said irritably. She had bargained with Hazard because he looked half sick to her, but she couldn't expect Dwayne to see that. All he saw was what he wanted to do. "Sometimes you act so spoiled," she said before she could stop herself, and then hurried off ahead of him.

"Hey boy!" Dwayne called, trotting along behind her, the popcorn bag clutched under his arm. "You mad with me, boy? You mad?"

Casey slowed down, thinking about what she could

say to him. "Just a little," she said finally. "Hazard wants to be married to Pansy just like you wanted to catch a lot of fish. Just like I want us always to be friends. It's important to him like that. And I want to help him because it's important to him. Do you understand, Dwayne?"

He stood grinning at her, then pushed the popcorn bag toward her. "Want some, boy?" he asked. "You're not mad at me anymore, are you?"

"No, Dwayne, I'm not mad." Casey brought out a fistful of popcorn, accepting the little gift he could offer her. But she couldn't believe he understood. She didn't know what love meant to him, how far beyond daily care and nourishment it went. Sure, he'd said he loved her yesterday, loved a boy, a friend. So easily he'd said those words she already found so difficult, sensing as she did, such commitment in them. Loving people was hard. It meant always trying to tell the truth. It meant figuring out when and how to give and take. Even love between friends meant that.

"Let's go watch a tent," she said.

PANSY WAS home when they got there, but she wasn't in the front yard ripping up the tent stakes or tossing Hazard's meager bedding in the trash can. Instead, she was standing on the porch talking to George Greenwald, the policeman Casey had met at the racetrack.

"Here they are," she said as Casey and Dwayne came across the lawn. "I just called the lumberyard," she said to Casey. "Your grandfather and Taylor will be here any minute. So will Jane."

"What is it?" Casey asked, her heart almost still with the dread that always struck first. "It's Daddy," she said.

"Oh no, dear. It's not about you. It's Dwayne," Pansy said, nervously fingering her brooch. "George here has a court order for him, signed by two doctors, one of which I'm ashamed to say is my own Dr. Kemble—what possessed him I'll never know—and, of course, the clerk of court." She shuddered out her breath, looking helplessly from Casey to Dwayne. "Alva Pickens is having him committed again."

Dwayne didn't seem to understand or else he wasn't listening. "The tent's still here," he said to Casey.

"You go watch it, Dwayne," Casey said. "In a minute Taylor and Grandpa will be here."

"They gonna watch it, too?" Dwayne scratched his head under his cap. He seemed to be refusing to acknowledge the policeman's presence or Pansy's frantic whispering.

Jane was puffing down the street. "I just went over to Dora's," she called, unable to hold back her news until she reached them. "She said Alva said it was the only thing to do since that fight he got into Saturday. She's distraught, poor woman, pulled between two sons like this. She doesn't want to let him go, but she wonders if it isn't the safest thing, the best thing for him. It's all for testing, you know. Of course, they've already tested him once and decided he was harmless, but that was before he took a swing at anybody." She had reached the porch and leaned against the rail, panting for breath. "My own opinion is that Alva's just been waiting for this. For something he could use to put that man away. Out of sight, out of mind. No blot on the royal family then. Sometimes I think Alva Pickens is the only person in this town who doesn't love Dwayne."

"I sure wish I wasn't having to do this," George said. He had his hat in his hand like he had come courting.

"We understand, George," Pansy said gently. "Better you than somebody who doesn't care about him."

"The worst of it is he'll have to stay in jail overnight. Somebody from the hospital is coming in the morning to get him."

"No," Casey muttered, surprised at her own self-control. She wanted to lash out, rip the papers from George's hand and tear them to shreds, but she just stood there staring at them and muttering, "No, no, no." They were adults. Why couldn't they be the ones saying no?

"Here's Taylor!" Dwayne called. "Hey Mr. Ben!"

"Hey Dwayne!" Taylor went right up on the porch and took the court order out of George's hand to study it.

"It's all legal, Taylor," George said. "Two doctors signed and the clerk of court. They examined him before he was taken up there the first time so they don't have to do it again. The clerk is a friend of Alva's, I reckon, because he sure as hell got this through fast. I got this thing about ten o'clock, but I just waited around, trying to think of something to do. Miss Pansy heard about it down at Dr. Kemble's and she came right home. Mrs. Pickens said Dwayne was over here, so this is where I ended up. Miss Pansy decided to call you." He stood breathlessly watching Taylor read the paper. "I don't think there's anything we can do."

"How long have we got?" Taylor asked.

"Somebody from the hospital is coming in the morning, but I have to take him into custody now. He'll have to spend the night in jail, but that gives us till morning to get this thing stopped. The law says this petition here can be withdrawn before the person is admitted to the institution, if the petitioner wants to."

"And the petitioner is Alva Pickens?" Taylor said. "I'll break every bone in his body."

"I think we better see a lawyer first," Ben said. "Right away. This afternoon."

"Well, I got to take Dwayne in, now that I've found him," George said. "His mama said he'd probably go with me all right as long as she wasn't around. She said she'd come down in the morning and see about him. That's who I feel sorry for," George said. "Mrs. Pickens don't want this to happen."

"Of course she doesn't," Jane said. "None of us do."

"I guess I'll tell him we're going for a ride in the police car," George said hesitantly. They were all looking out in the yard where Dwayne was tossing an imaginary ball and running, head back, to catch it.

"No," Casey said. "Don't lie to him."

"I'll go down with you," Taylor said. "I'll explain about going to see the lawyer. I'll tell him he won't have to go to the hospital." He rammed the porch post with his fist. "And that damn well better turn out to be the truth."

"I want to come," Casey said.

"No. Just tell him you'll see him tomorrow," Taylor said firmly.

"You might cry, honey," Jane said. "We all might, and that wouldn't help Dwayne a bit."

"Dwayne!" George called. "Listen here, boy!"

Dwayne stopped playing and stood between the porch and the patrol car.

"I got this paper here," George began reluctantly. "It's a paper about your going to the hospital for a little while—Oh, hell, Taylor, you tell him."

Taylor was already in the yard, his arm firmly around Dwayne's shoulder while Dwayne stood like a submissive child who expected punishment but couldn't remember his crime.

"It's because of the fight, Dwayne," Taylor said. "It's because you helped me out."

Dwayne grinned. "We got 'em all right," he said. Then he frowned. "But I didn't like fighting much."

"I know," Taylor said. "And that's what I'm going to tell our lawyer and the judge and the doctors and everybody in town, if I have to. But meanwhile you have to spend the rest of today and probably tonight down at the jail. That's what George's paper tells him to do."

"Take me away?" Dwayne asked. "It says to take me off somewhere, George?" he called, panic rising in his voice. He pulled away from Taylor. "It's like that other time, ain't it? I don't want to go there again, I told you that. I told everybody. I told you that, didn't I, K.C.? I can't have a radio there or a ball, even. I just sit there, waiting all day, and nothin' happens. I don't want to go there."

"You won't have to. I promise," Taylor said. "But right now, while I'm getting it fixed, you have to go downtown with George. I'll go with you."

But Dwayne was intent on talking them out of it. If

he could just keep talking, keep finding words to tell them why he couldn't go, it would be all right. They would understand and believe him. "K.C. and me were gonna play ball. We got to watch this tent, you see, so Miss Pansy don't tear it down, and we were gonna play ball while we watched it."

"I'll watch it, Dwayne," Casey called from the porch. She couldn't go any closer because she was crying. Tears spread their distorting film across her eyes and mucus trickled down one nostril. "I'll be right here when you get back."

He didn't understand why they were so far away, on the porch like that. Miss Jane and Mr. Ben, even Miss Pansy—why, they all knew him! They knew how he hated that place. "I don't want to go!" he yelled.

"Taylor'll fix it, Dwayne," Miss Jane called back. "You go ahead now, and don't be worried."

George went down to the car and opened the door so that Dwayne and Taylor could get in. The people on the porch were silent, watching the scene as if it were just that, a scene being acted with the clear knowledge of everybody concerned that it was only a play.

"Well, they're gone," Pansy said when the car had pulled away.

"Taylor will get it straightened out," Jane said. "I'm sure it can be worked out."

"We shouldn't have let him go," Casey said coldly. She refused to look at any of them. They were adults, they knew how to do things. They should have kept Dwayne safe. If they couldn't, then who could?

"Oh, Casey, you'll be learning there's little justice in this world," Pansy said wearily. "There's little that's fair." She sat down on the swing, her hands folded, and looked out at the tent in her yard.

"He'll be all right, honey." Jane tried to put her arms around the girl, but Casey pulled away.

"No, he won't. He'll be down there in the jail and he'll be scared all by himself and he'll be trying to figure out why we just stood here, letting him go," Casey said bitterly. She was holding back her tears, too angry to give way again. "We know him, Grandma! How could we let him go when we know him!"

"She's right," Pansy said. "Casey's right."

"Taylor's doing all that can be done. We just have to wait."

"Casey," Pansy said, "I want you to take that tent down."

"No!" She was staring at the road as if by closely watching she could turn today into tomorrow and have the car return with Dwayne still in it, never alone or frightened. "No, I won't."

"You are right, Casey, what you said about our knowing Dwayne," Pansy said softly, gently, as if she understood Casey's anger and could wait a long time for it to subside. "It's the same with Hazard and me. How could I let him go when I know him? How could I?"

So, later that afternoon, when Hazard came to Pansy's yard after work, the tent was gone. Only a rectangle of browning grass remained to commemorate his vigil. He stood in the yard, facing his defeat wearily, unable to think beyond this moment when his life seemed so wasted, so doomed to loneliness.

"Hazard," Pansy said from the doorway. She was standing behind the screen but he could see her, the outline of her fine figure imprinted against the waning afternoon light. "Come in."

He was afraid to move. What if his legs would no longer carry him? What if, this close, he stumbled?

"I don't ever want to hurt you again," he heard himself say. His voice lifted over the porch hedge, wafted against her house, her screen, her heart.

"I know you, Hazard Whitaker," she said, "and you are worth the risk."

⋫ *17* ⋪

The day dragged on.
Casey fiddled with her lunch, but Jane didn't reprimand her. What was the use? Nobody felt like eating.

"I think I'll leave the dishes," Jane said. "I feel so drained this afternoon." She draped her apron over a chair and gave the cluttered counter around the sink a frown. She had expected Casey to offer to do the kitchen.

But Casey was silent. She stared at the melting ice in her glass of tea, refusing to look at her grandmother. They had all failed Dwayne, and she couldn't tell them it was all right. That was what doing the dishes would mean—that she was willing to let the day go on like any other day, doing chores upon which daily life subsisted, pretending nothing was amiss.

She wouldn't pretend she could trust them, either, she was thinking as the door swung shut behind her grandmother. And if you couldn't trust grown-ups who wrote and understood the laws, then who could you trust? And what about Taylor, mad as a hornet, but still not doing anything after he'd promised her he would? Talking to a lawyer. What good would that do when Mr. Greenwald said the papers were all in order? It was all legal for them to take Dwayne off to jail like he was a criminal. She expected more of Taylor than that. Of her grandparents. Even of Pansy and Hazard. They should never have let Dwayne go. They had all failed him. All of them, including herself.

She had thought, standing with them on Pansy's porch that morning and watching Dwayne and Taylor disappear into the patrol car, that what was going on was beyond her ability to prevent. She had muttered, subdued by an appalling willingness to let it happen, when she could have shouted.

All it would have taken was her yelling, "Run!" or, "Don't let them take you!" and chances were Dwayne would have done what she told him. That was what he'd wanted, someone to say, "This is wrong and we won't let it happen."

She'd heard sermons about such situations at chapel with half the congregation in uniform and the chaplain talking about duty, the distinctions between right and wrong, responsibility. But the chaplain wore a uniform himself under his vestments, and duty was always against a hypothetical enemy, some unidentified evil without a name or face. Moral conscience always meant country, democracy, the rights of men to govern themselves in these lectures that laced ideals with flowery language until the ideals themselves seemed vague and impractical, outside the reach of women and children. She had heard those sermons, listening with half an ear and absorbing only because of the constancy of the subject—sooner or later, you had to hear. But never before had she put real people to the principle, never had she cast the show with actors whose voices curled off the stage like empty, useless whiffs of smoke. "Just tell him you'll see him tomorrow." . . . "You have to go,

Dwayne." . . . "It's because of the fight." . . . "I'll watch the tent." Those faces on the porch—those people she had all summer been learning to depend on—they were the enemy, although she hadn't seen that until it was too late and Pansy was telling her to take the tent down. Pansy was taking Hazard back while they were abandoning Dwayne.

She got up and stuck her glass among the dirty dishes, then went out the back door. The afternoon was still with a breathless, vacant kind of heat, deathlike. People were napping, probably even Dwayne's mother, who had convinced herself there was nothing to do but continue with her day as if nothing were wrong.

Casey could see the empty lot through the trees. She felt a longing, as her body ached with muscles held too tight, to hear the thud of a baseball against Dwayne's drum. She went across the street and pushed against the door of his garage. In the hazy, warm dark she made out a rack of bats against the wall, and rummaging around it, she found the box of balls and collected some.

Out on the lot she took the mound. Dwayne never let her pitch, but she had watched him so often that the moves, although awkward, came to her. She watched the first ball glance off the metal near the base of the drum.

"Strike one!" she shouted.

The second pitch was more solid and nearer the center of the drum. "It's a base hit!" she screamed, dashing after the grounder.

She was beginning to sweat. Hatless, she squinted at the plate and let go another pitch that missed the drum altogether and rolled into the weeds along the fence. "Damn!" she shouted. "Damn, damn, damn!" Tears mixed with sweat on her cheeks, and she wiped her grimy hand across her face while she went after the ball.

Back on the mound, she went on pitching, calling the plays, retrieving the balls. Her arms began to pinch, stinging at the joints, but still she threw the ball because she had to be doing something, even if it were nothing. Even if it didn't help. She knew there was no redeeming her silence on the porch, but still she pitched, her body straining against its private inner ache because she had failed Dwayne Pickens.

Across the street, awakened from a restless doze by a familiar yet incongruous sound, Jane Flanagan stood at her kitchen door and watched, her own heart aching, as the girl burned out the rage they all shared but could not express.

"Oh, Casey," she said aloud.

The metallic thump of the baseball gave the neighborhood a new pulse, a heavy, lonely, throbbing sound. All through the long afternoon it toned, like a knelling bell, their lethargy, their indifference, their unspeakable failure, until Casey was exhausted and flung herself on the Flanagans' porch, her body heavy with sweat and dust.

She was too tired to resist her grandmother's folding arms around her, and so, her head heavy with heat, she leaned into the comfort she had all afternoon rejected, and whispered, "We have to get him back. We have to."

"We will, Casey. I promise." Jane stroked her damp, fragile head.

"We were wrong to let him go," Casey said.

"We were wrong, but I believe he will forgive us."

"But I won't, Grandma. I'll never forgive myself."

Jane held her, unable to say that age had taught her how people do forgive, even forget, the wrongs they've done. It was, she knew, one of the blessings of life, that lessening of pain by time until grief, once so vile a wound, was eventually a tiny scar, the result of slow, silent healing.

Still, at that moment, the wound was too deep for reason, and so she listened as Casey repeated the word over and over, a litany of remorse: "Never, never, never," knowing that there was no comfort beyond arms that held gently, restfully, accepting both the guilt and the love she now knew her grandchild capable of.

It WAS after six when Taylor came home from the afternoon spent at the jail and in the lawyer's office. He dropped into a kitchen chair while the rest of the family clustered around him waiting to hear.

"George was right," he said finally. "The only way to stop them from taking Dwayne tomorrow is to stop Alva. I called his office ten times this afternoon but he's always out."

"Conveniently, I suppose," Ben said. "Well, we'll have to find him tonight."

"But that means Dwayne will have to spend the night in jail," Casey protested.

"I'm afraid so, honey, but I don't think that matters to him as much as staying out of the hospital does. He knows the hospital means a long time." Taylor took her hand. "We'll get him back," he said. "I mean that. I just don't know how yet."

"First we have to find Alva," Ben said, going to the telephone.

"Marge doesn't know where he is now," he said when he returned, "but she said he'd be at the town meeting at seven o'clock. I can't believe we elected that man to the town board."

"Then we'll go to the town meeting," Jane said. "That's a better place than most to confront him."

"Second only to the churchyard," Taylor said, beginning to smile.

"But how can the town meeting stop him?" Casey wanted to know.

"I don't know that it will," Jane said. "But it's worth a try, don't you think, Ben? There's no changing Alva's mind in private, we already know that much. He always was a stubborn, conceited boy. He'll have to be shamed into withdrawing that petition. Just what would embarrass him even more than having Dwayne loose?"

"Having the whole town know he was putting him away, that's what," Ben said. "He thought he could do it on the sly like the last time when he caught us napping."

"Well, I think we can wake them up tonight," Taylor said. He was feeling better. "Let's eat."

"So we'll go to the town meeting," Jane said. She busied herself with getting sandwiches on the table. "We'll all go." She smiled at Casey. "All the Flanagans."

The town meeting was already in progress when they got there. The Flanagans sat down behind the fifty or so citizens in the audience to get the gist of the proceedings. The mayor and six aldermen were sitting behind a table with stacks of papers in front of them. One of them was writing frantically. Smoke clouded the air above the table.

A black woman in the audience was addressing the men. She stood straight, her arms folded across her stomach, her flowered summer hat quivering as she moved her head emphatically. Only her head moved as she told them how the sewer system in her part of town was leaking again, the recent patching job having lasted only long enough for the construction company to collect their checks.

"We got sewage in the street," she was saying, her eyes flashing but her body still and her voice hushed because she knew the risk she was taking by being there at all. "We got a stench in our streets. We got children locked inside their houses in the hot summertime to keep them out of the mess bubbling up. But the smell comes in the house at us, anyways."

"Mr. Mayor!" One of the aldermen leaned down the table toward the mayor. "Harley, we got people coming at us every whipstitch wanting this and wanting that." He straightened up to look out at the woman. "Everybody needs something, woman."

"Hear her out," the mayor said. "Let's hear her out." He was smiling. "She pays town taxes just like you and me, even if she don't pay much. All according as they're able," he ended sanctimoniously.

Another alderman cleared his throat in preparation to saying something. Everybody waited. "We got that sewer system put in down there in colored town," he said in a slow, mournful drawl. "We got it in there where they didn't have nothin' but a slop jar and a outhouse. What I want to know is, ain't they ever satisfied?" He peered at the black woman.

"We're mothers here, speaking to you about our children," she said in a deep throaty voice. "We got hot weather and flies. We got sickness coming if it ain't cleaned up. We can't clean it up by ourselves. We're here about our children."

"That's right, Emmaline," one of the other women said. Emmaline sat down, her hat still shaking, while the women around her nodded, commending her performance as they watched with bitter, glancing looks at the men who mumbled among themselves at the table.

"Well," the mayor said, puffing himself up for a little speech. "I've contacted the company. They've been informed of the problem down there. They say they'll be in there doing something later this week."

"They promised that last week!" one of the women said, shaking her finger at the aldermen while the women next to her tried to ease her agitation by patting her shoulder and taking her hand.

"This is a firm commitment," the mayor said calmly. "We are doing the best we can, ladies." He smiled down at them, thinking he had appeased them by calling them ladies.

Seeing a break in the proceedings, Taylor stood up.

"State the nature of your business, Mr. Flanagan," the clerk called, glad to see a white man to contend with. Here was a friend, someone with more important business than a little leak in the sewer line.

"Personal, Howard," Taylor said firmly. "And then again, not so personal. I'm here about an issue that has to do with us as people. It's as serious as sewage and about as hard to get rid of."

The black women nodded and smiled, happy he was respecting their situation.

Alva Pickens leaned back in his chair and eyed Taylor over his glasses. He sensed the nature of Taylor's business, having noted the Flanagan contingency from the moment they arrived, but he thought it better to sit it out. Let Taylor make a fool of himself and then Alva could use the situation to his own advantage. He knew how to turn a situation to his advantage. It made him a good businessman and an even better politician.

"Today a court order was signed committing Dwayne Pickens to a mental institution," Taylor said forcefully. "It was signed by two doctors who examined him five years ago. It was also signed by the clerk of court and by the petitioner, Alva Pickens, Dwayne's brother." Taylor paused and looked around the room. He wanted to be sure everybody was paying attention. He needed everybody in the room rooting for Dwayne just like they would were he a great baseball player or the best racer on the track. Feet shuffled and people turned in their folding chairs to get a clearer view of the speaker.

"Now we all know Dwayne," Taylor went on.

"We do!" the black women sang out.

"We know him because he's been free to walk our streets, shop in our stores, attend our public functions for thirty years. He's even provided some public functions of his own with his baseball games. He's always been respectful. More than that, he's been good-natured in the face of taunting from certain quarters."

"That's right! I've seen it!" a white man across the aisle said. "He's good-hearted all right!"

"Now we know Dwayne's mind is not quite right. We know he's slow. But a lot of us are not as quick as we ought to be!"

The audience chuckled while Taylor got his breath. He could feel them with him. They were remembering Dwayne, each of them recalling those little encounters they hadn't even noticed at the time, his way of greeting them, his loose, careless gait, his unabashed enthusiasm that made them smile.

"The fact is Dwayne got into a little fight at the racetrack last Saturday. I guess you can see by my appearance, so did I." He touched his bruised cheek gingerly. "I was the cause of the fight, but nobody's locked me up. The fact is I called on Dwayne when things got a little thick out there."

Some of the men chuckled again, and Taylor flashed them a quick smile.

"God knows, Dwayne's got a swing. There's no denying that. But he didn't start that fight and when it was over, he threw up all over my trailer. It made him sick to hit a man. That's what he said.

"Now Alva Pickens here wants us to think Dwayne is dangerous. He wants us to treat him like he's a crazy person. Right this minute, Dwayne is over there locked up in jail for no good reason that I can think of. Dwayne doesn't understand why he's there and neither do I."

"Why is he, Alva?" a woman said from the audience. She popped her gum loudly and pressed her pocketbook to her bosom.

The audience and the alderman were staring at Alva,

who was refusing to look at anybody. He polished his glasses slowly to prove his control, put them back on his nose carefully, and then leaned over to speak to the men at the other end of the table. "This is a personal matter," he began. "I believe Mr. Flanagan is out of order."

"You're the one that's out of order," a new voice said from the audience. It was the barber Casey had seen that day. "Why, I've been cutting Dwayne Pickens's hair all these years. There's nothing dangerous about that boy. Nothing wrong with him except he acts like a kid." The man nodded at the Flanagans.

"That's right," the gum-chewing woman said. "I work the concessions at the picture show, and he's never caused no trouble there. Why, there's kids in there spilling all over everything, yellin' and carryin' on, them what ain't neckin' to beat the band. But not Dwayne. He's looking at the picture, I can promise you that." She sat back, satisfied.

"I know him, too," the mayor said, grinning down at the barber. "Met him just this morning."

"Mr. Mayor," Taylor thundered, seeing the point beginning to slip away. "I've come here tonight, understanding the terms and conditions of this petition Alva Pickens has signed against his brother. I've come knowing that the board of aldermen cannot stop this action any more than the Flanagans or God Almighty Himself can. But I've promised that boy he will not be sent away from his home, from his town, from the people who care about him. I'm not ashamed to say I love Dwayne Pickens. We grew up together. I know him, and I believe he has a right to reap the rewards of living in this fine community as much as you or I do."

"Amen!" the women chorused.

"It's for his own good," Alva said stonily, unable to tolerate dissent any longer. He pounded the table with his fist, betraying the frustration he'd felt mounting ever since Dwayne took his car. "I don't know what to do with him!"

"You don't have to do anything with him, Alva," Taylor said. "You never did. He's as much our brother as he is yours."

"Mama won't live forever," Alva said, wearily trying another tactic. He snorted into his handkerchief. "Mrs. Flanagan, you understand, don't you? You know how Mama takes care of him. What's going to become of him when she's gone? Who's going to be responsible then?"

"I don't know, Alva," Jane Flanagan said, rising to stand beside her son. "But why make him start living such a sad life before he has to? It'll come soon enough. He's a happy person, Alva. Let him have that much now, no matter what there is to come. No matter what you think is best for him."

"What can I do?" Alva moaned, slumping in his chair.

"First thing in the morning, you go back to the clerk of court and withdraw this petition," George Greenwald said, having just entered from the back. "You have to get the written consent of the doctors who signed this thing in the first place, and then the clerk of court will write up a motion dropping the whole business."

"How's Dwayne?" Casey called. "Is he all right, Mr. Greenwald?"

"Sleeping like a baby," George said. "I stayed right in there with him till he was asleep. He knows we're getting him out of there. I can tell he believes it."

"He's got more faith in human nature than I do," the mayor said. "A whole lot more."

Alva sat up straight again, as if he'd gotten a second wind. "I tell you, you people are mingling in something that's none of your business," he said, looking from the mayor to the Flanagans.

"What we've come here to tell you, Alva," Taylor said patiently, "is that Dwayne *is* our business."

"All you got to do is make a phone call, Alva," the mayor said. "That's all it'll take, isn't that right, George?"

"Yes sir. That's all. Just one little ol' telephone call to the clerk's office and he'll take care of the rest. I'm sure of that."

"Well, do *something*, Alva," one of the aldermen said, "or we'll be here all night!"

Alva looked around the table and then out at the audience as if he were tallying the opposition. He stood up, scraping his chair heavily. "I don't know what I'm going to do about Dwayne, but right now, I'm going home. And don't you come badgering me, Taylor Flanagan. I've seen enough fools for one night!" He slammed his hat on his head and marched out the side door.

"Hope he doesn't look in the mirror," Taylor said. The audience laughed with relief.

"Do you think he'll keep the boy home?" the mayor asked in the direction of the Flanagans.

"I think he will, Harley," Ben said. "I've known Alva

Pickens since the day he was born and he's not all bad."

"Just about half," the barber said.

"I think he's been shamed into keeping Dwayne home. I truly do," Jane said, hugging Casey to her. "We can pray for it now because we've done all we can do ourselves."

Casey was feeling better. She grabbed Taylor around the neck and kissed his uninjured cheek with a loud smack. "I just wish Gwen had been here to see you," she said. "You ought to be a preacher."

"That's what I told him when he was a little boy," Jane said. "Looks like it finally took on him! Now let's go on home and get to bed. Dwayne's going to be the only person around here getting a good night's sleep."

"But what about tomorrow?" Casey asked, following her grandmother outside.

"Tomorrow we'll just have to see if Alva has any redeeming qualities," Jane said.

"And if he doesn't, I intend to rearrange his face," Taylor added.

CASEY WENT with Taylor to the jail the next morning. They didn't see Alva's Chrysler but they hurried inside anyway, Casey's empty stomach fluttering as she tightened her grip on Taylor's hand.

"Maybe he called," Taylor said, but Casey could see he was worried.

"He did it!" George said in the doorway. "I sure had my doubts, but he called just a little while ago. The clerk's over at the Courthouse getting the consents ready for the doctors. You can take him on because they'll both sign. I don't think they wanted any part of this business to begin with." He was grinning and he slapped Taylor on the back. "He's waiting for somebody to come get him. He's wanting to see you."

George hurried off as Casey let go of Taylor's hand and stood absolutely still, oblivious to the activity around her, waiting to see Dwayne come through the door. When he came, Casey was the first person he focused on, like the rest of them weren't even there.

"Hey boy," he called.

"Hey Dwayne," she answered. "You're coming home now. Your mama's waiting for you at your house, and Grandma's making a big cake and we're going to have a party tonight!"

"A party! *Wow-weeee!*" Dwayne slapped his thigh with his cap.

"Fried chicken, too, because I told Grandma that's your favorite."

" 'Bye!" Dwayne said to the officers in the station. "I'm going on home now. 'Bye!"

They climbed into Taylor's car and pulled away just as a state car pulled in behind them. "They're in for a surprise," Taylor said, looking through his rear-view mirror at the two men getting out. "Maybe they'll take Alva instead."

"We got to watch that tent today, K.C.?" Dwayne wanted to know.

"Nope, it's gone."

"Miss Pansy tore it down?" Dwayne looked distressed. "I told you all I had to watch it."

"It's not because we didn't watch it, Dwayne. It's because Hazard got Pansy back, just like he wanted to.

And we got you back, just like we wanted to." Casey had to resist her impulse to hug him.

"And I got you all back, too," Dwayne said, grinning. "Now let's us play some baseball!"

⇒ *18* ⇐

*C*asey *felt the pain* behind her eyes long before she opened them. She lay perfectly still, wishing the pain away while it crept across her temples, behind her ears, and into her neck.

I'll go back to sleep, she thought, and when I wake up it will be gone.

She dozed.

The air around her was warm and moist, too thick to breathe normally. She began to take shallow, light breaths that didn't hurt so much. She relaxed a little.

I'm tired, she thought, remembering that they had brought Dwayne home just yesterday and there had been a party last night.

She tried to remember the party, but her head hurt too much. Before her closed eyes moved quick, erratic pictures: Taylor and Gwen dancing the shag, Gwen's skirt floating out and then settling against her puffy white crinoline; her grandmother bustling between the kitchen and the dining room, Dora Pickens trailing after her wanting to be helpful; Hazard and Pansy looking at each other across the room, smiles hovering above their coffee cups; Dwayne, sprawled on the sofa watching everything and slapping his knees, calling to Gwen to dance with him, then his mama, then even her grandmother, who blushed and did a little Charleston step across the living-room floor. Dwayne happy. Dwayne rescued. Dwayne wrapped in love.

She was so hot. She wanted to get up and stir the air with her body. She wanted to move, but she didn't. She opened her eyes. The room was the same. The morning had broken over it as always, the same white spots across her daddy's desk, the same thin trickle of morning beneath her shade. The pain in her head made her vision blur. It hurt so bad. She wanted to pound her temples to make it stop, but still she didn't move.

In a minute I'll get up, she thought, pushing her mind to reason beyond the hot rushes of pain that swept through her on every swift, panting breath.

I'll be all right, she thought, closing her eyes. I'll stay here until it goes away. Minutes passed. She tried to turn over, but her head hurt too much. Her arms seemed heavy, elephantine.

She needed to go to the bathroom. It was a clear sensation, the only painless, natural feeling she could recognize. She felt such relief.

I'll go to the bathroom and then I'll be all right, she thought. She tried to smile, wanting to display her relief in some concrete fashion, but her cheeks were too dry and her skin too tight. The smile refused to come.

Suddenly she knew she couldn't move. Without even testing her legs and trunk, she knew. Her mouth opened, formed a silent, hollow O. She closed her eyes again, closed her mind against the sound she was so afraid to hear.

They heard her scream in the kitchen. It was not the

high-pitched, shrill screech of acute pain, but a throaty resigned cry of defeat. They went to her, Jane with her face ashen, aged by thirty seconds of despair between kitchen and bedroom; Ben, calm but with his breakfast napkin still tucked into his shirt; Taylor, racing ahead of them, believing he could and would conquer whatever awaited them.

Casey opened her eyes. They were there, leaning over her. Hands she couldn't feel touched her forehead, her arms, her hot bare legs.

"It hurts," she whispered through dry lips.

"Call Dr. Kemble," Jane said, her face set against her fear. "Get the thermometer, Taylor. And a pan of cool water." She had to be doing something. She knew there was nothing to do, but she would perform the rituals of care anyway.

Casey felt the cool water on her face. It dribbled down her neck and she opened her mouth and bit down on the towel, sucking moisture onto her tongue. The pain seemed better. Having them there gave her something else to concentrate on. She wanted them to stay with her, but she was afraid to try to say it. What if she couldn't? She wouldn't try. She fell asleep.

Dr. Kemble came and with him, Pansy and Hazard. They sat on the porch waiting while the doctor went upstairs. He was back again too soon, before they were prepared to hear.

"I don't know," the doctor said to them in the front hallway. "There are, of course, polio symptoms—high fever, pain, stiff joints, poor body movement. At the same time, I've seen some influenza cases like this. Polio is a virus, you know. It attacks the cells in the central nervous system. How strong the virus is determines how many cells it attacks. A few cells, a light case. A lot of cells, a severe case. That's about all we know. Other viruses can have the same primary symptoms. Unfortunately, only time will tell. If it's a simple virus, she could be well in three or four days. Even with a mild case of polio, she could be much better in the same length of time and with little or no permanent damage." He hesitated and then shook his head wearily. "God knows, I wish I could tell you something else. Someday there'll be a way to fight this thing, but I know that's little comfort now. I'll come back around noon. Try to get the fever down with alcohol rubs and sponge baths. Pay close attention to her breathing. If she starts gasping, call an ambulance. Otherwise we'll try to keep her out of the hospital."

"We'll take turns," Pansy said when the doctor had gone. "Two-hour shifts staying with her."

"I can't leave her now," Jane said. She hurried back up the stairs with Ben following her.

"You'd better stay, Pansy," Taylor said. "We're going to need both of you before this is over."

Pansy and Hazard cleared the kitchen. The familiar work calmed them a little, put a simple form of normalcy into their day. But they were silent. Hazard watched Pansy's narrow wrists dip into the suds in the dishpan. He saw the soft rise of her breasts as she drew quick breaths. He heard the sighs that floated between them like a dismal melody. Finally, he took her hand, drew it out of the soapy water so it appeared pink and dripping between them, and dried it carefully, touching her as lightly as he could.

"We're together," he said. "We can do whatever we have to do now. We can help them."

"But we can't save Casey," Pansy said. She was beginning to cry as she put her head against him.

"No, but we mustn't underestimate her, either."

"Oh, Hazard, don't you understand, there's nothing we can do, there's nothing she can do," Pansy moaned tearfully. "There's nothing anybody can do."

"I don't believe that," Hazard said, lifting her face to his. "Not any more. We are proof, Pansy, that people can do something."

"I wish it were that simple," Pansy said, trying to smile at him.

"There's nothing simple about it," Hazard said. "All I know is she's got to want to get well, we've got to make sure she wants it bad enough, no matter how she's hurting."

Ben came into the kitchen.

"How is she?" Pansy and Hazard asked together.

"The same. She sleeps and then wakes up for a minute. It's like she's unconscious most of the time. Jane is sponging her off, but she moans through it like the water hurts her. I don't think it's doing any good." He sat down in a chair and rested his head on the heels of his hands. "We shouldn't have let her go places like we did. Down at the racetrack every Saturday. She went to the beach just a couple of days ago. All over town with Dwayne Pickens. We should have kept her home."

Pansy was silent, thinking to herself that he was probably right.

"I know it doesn't do any good for me to say you

shouldn't blame yourself," Hazard said, "but I don't see how you could have prevented this, seeing how the doctors don't even know how people get it."

"Hazard's right, Daddy," Taylor said from the doorway. His face was splotched but he didn't seem to care that they could see he'd been crying. "We just have to make her as comfortable as we can. And pray it's not polio."

"I'll go help Jane," Pansy said. She wanted to leave the men alone together, comforting each other with the silence that was familiar between them.

Upstairs she paused in the open doorway of Casey's room to watch Jane bending over the still body, the white narrow bed. Jane was pressing a cloth to Casey's neck and shoulders, then dipping it back into the pan of water, squeezing it so a trickle of water fell back into the pan, then pressing the girl's skin once more.

She moved silently about her task, her head bent, body intent on this saving, this salvaging of a life so close to her own. Nothing else mattered. Nothing counted but the woman and the child, the precious cooling of one body with the skill of another, the laying on of hands.

THE DAYS seemed endless, but for Jane Flanagan it was the nights, the sheer hot panic that came when no one was awake but her, which brought the most relentless terror. She would sit there beside the bed, listening to the breathing, hearing it closer than her own, and would think through the crucial days of her life, reacquainting herself with old griefs, remembering survivals and losses.

Illnesses spread themselves before her like languishing demons. Deaths draped their heavy shrouds around the dark room. Sometimes she cried. Just sitting there, her hand resting close to her grandchild's limp fingers —just in case—she would let the tears held back all that day come, spilling down her cold, determined cheeks. Nothing had prepared her for this.

She had not reached Barbara yet, but she knew she hadn't tried very hard, at least not since that first day. She didn't want to call her at work, so she'd tried at suppertime and then late at night when Barbara should be home from her second job, but wasn't. She'd let the phone ring for minutes, hearing it fill the hollow, vacant house so far away, until the operator cut in with her crisp, official, "Would you like to try again?" So Jane had waited another day, another little while, because she couldn't find words—she who was so quick with words—to tell a mother that her daughter might die.

For two days and nights she'd waited, doubting the possibility of a break in the fever, although Dr. Kemble came confidently morning and evening, telling her how the limbs were no worse, how the effectiveness of the alcohol rubs against the fever was a good sign, how Casey would not die. Jane didn't believe him. As much as she wanted Casey to live, as surely as she knew she would change places if she could, she felt somehow resigned.

It was as if knowing she herself could not make Casey live meant the child was doomed. Everything had rested in her hands for so long. Every comfort, every need of her family had been hers to offer, her sustaining gift to those she loved, until she couldn't believe they could succeed outside her will, outside her determined pursuit of their happiness.

Now everything was out of control. All those little things, like the small domestic tasks she'd always relished, had gone haywire; bigger things had, too, like Dwayne Pickens knowing Casey was a girl. She hadn't expected that to happen, not this late in the summer when Casey had put such effort into keeping her secret. Jane had even helped her by going to Dora Pickens that first day and explaining the circumstances of her granddaughter's lie, justifying a deed she had never expected to find justifiable.

But now he knew because he had been sitting on the front porch that first evening, waiting with the rest of them to hear how Casey was. He had been on the stoop, his back to them, when the doctor came out and stood in the patch of hall light on the porch like he intended to give a recitation.

"She's just the same," was all he'd said. "She's a sick little girl, but I think we have good reason to believe she'll pull through."

So Dwayne heard, and because the doctor's news was no news at all, Jane had looked at Dwayne instead, had seen him rise off the stoop like some threatened, angered monster, seen him flailing the air in the darkening front yard, his head back like a dog ready to howl at the moon, but silent, mute while his mind circled the truth. Casey was a girl. He loved a girl!

• 19 •

*T*he fever took Casey in and out like a swinging door that slammed back in her face, having given her a glimpse of a cool place, a quiet, restful, shaded spot under the tree in her backyard at home.

She had the only full-grown tree on the block because the military bulldozer had plowed through the housing development site as if it had been commanded to obliterate every sign of life. Somehow, one straggly sweet gum had survived, refused to lie down and die under a pile of red clay, so Casey had a real tree while the neighbors struggled with dogwoods and flowering fruit trees still staked up after all these years.

In her fog of fever, she saw the tree like a mirage, shimmering and not quite there. Her head tossed on the pillow as she fought to keep the door open a little longer. She wanted to see the tree. She knew the full-leafed branches would cool her. She knew that if they would just take her home to the tree, she would be all right.

But the door slammed; the deep, leafy illusion was gone. Her mouth was dry and she couldn't swallow.

"I don't think she's breathing right," she heard someone saying. It was Pansy, her voice throbbing anxiously at Casey's temples.

"Sh-h-h."

The scent of alcohol stung her nostrils.

"It's all right, Casey. Just rest easy, honey."

She stopped trying to swallow. Saliva formed around her tongue. It seemed to be filling up her mouth. She would drown if she didn't swallow. She felt her throat opening and swallowed involuntarily, easily, without the gagging effort she'd expected.

"She's easier now," a voice said. But Casey knew it wasn't so.

SHE WAS cooler. Sunk like a stone deep within her empty gut, she sensed a coolness, felt it slowly begin to rise, floating inside her hollow stomach, pushing moisture to her skin's dry, shrunken surface. She felt slightly damp. The hot, dry bed seemed to draw at her flesh, collecting in tiny wet spots behind her knees and along her neck.

"Drink," she murmured, not opening her eyes. She knew someone was there.

A straw pushed itself between her lips and struck her teeth as she grasped it and sucked. The liquid spewed around her mouth, trickled down her throat. She gagged and coughed, her body heaving forward, her head spinning as it came off the pillow toward a hand raised in front of her. She opened her eyes. Taylor was holding her. He took her shoulders in his firm hands and lifted her against his chest, away from the wet bed and the dank, hot smell of her own body.

"I can move," she whispered into his chest.

"Of course you can," he said.

She could feel his chest, the heavy shuddering breaths he drew as he nursed her head, fingers at her dry, itching scalp, his arms enfolding her like her daddy's would.

"Mama. Daddy." Just the sound of the words made her heave again, but this time a sob came up, a plaintive whimpering sob that made Taylor want to cry himself.

"He's in Korea, Casey," he said. "Remember? You're here with us now."

Another sob came, and then another. Her body retched with sobs, her face and chest were sweaty with tears and the salty moisture that oozed up out of her skin.

"You're going to be all right, Casey," Taylor said, rocking her against his chest. "You can move. See?" He lifted her arm before her face. "You can feel." He rubbed her arm gently. "You can feel that, Casey. I know you can."

"What is it?" Jane was in the doorway, her face drawn and shadowed.

"She's cooler, Mama." Taylor lay her gently back on the bed. "She's sweating a lot and I think she can move all her limbs. Can you move your legs, Casey? Try to, Casey."

They were bending over her anxiously, their faces betraying the hours of torment she hadn't known existed. She was so tired, though. The damp bed seemed to pull at her, reminding her of sleep.

"Try, Casey, try."

She squeezed her eyes tightly shut, sending all her energy down her legs. Her foot moved. She felt the slight pressure of the sheet on her toes. Her ankle bent. There seemed to be pulse in her calves, a dull, throbbing ache that took all her strength to combat.

"She's all right!" Taylor said.

"Go back to sleep, honey," her grandmother said close to her face. "We'll be right here."

She felt fingers against her palm, trembling fingers spilling out their joy into her hand. She clutched the fingers to still them in hers, and went to sleep.

DWAYNE CAME. She was cool by then, the bed changed to crisp, dry sheets that didn't smell of fever; but still she didn't want to move, knowing she could. She was too tired. She saw him in the doorway, his baseball cap in his hand, the other hand behind his back, his head ducked in an embarrassed, hesitant tilt.

"Hey," she said softly.

"Hey boy," he said and came a little way into the room. He didn't look around but stared straight at her, as if her face were the proof he needed that she was all right.

"I knew you were gonna get well," he blurted out, "because I prayed for you, goddammit!" He grinned and slapped his cap against his thigh.

"Come sit down," she said, trying to put a familiar, healthy sound in her voice for him. She wanted to be just the way he remembered.

"Here," he said, thrusting a handful of daisies at her. Some of the stems stuck out from the squashed bundle. "I picked them all along the ditch bank. They grow wild, you know. Ain't no store-bought flowers."

"They're nice, Dwayne," she said, taking the flowers against her chest.

"Girls like flowers," Dwayne said. He put his baseball cap back on, but far back so that the bill stood straight up and she could see his face clearly. "I know you're a girl, Casey," he said.

"You didn't have to come see me," she said. Her eyes brimmed with tears that seemed too close lately, so eager. She wiped them away with her free hand. "I would understand if you didn't ever want to see me again."

Dwayne frowned, trying to figure out what she meant. "Sure I want to see you," he said. "We gonna play baseball all next week, but if you can't, we'll go to the show and to the racetrack and everything. Just like always, Casey. I want everything to be like always."

"But I'm a girl," Casey said. "And you don't like girls."

"Shoot!" Dwayne bobbed his head and then looked at her shyly. "You don't know nothin'! How you know that? How you know what Dwayne Pickens likes and don't like?"

Casey was silent, wishing she had an answer.

"Now you get well, you hear?" Dwayne was saying. He patted his foot restlessly and then stood up and pushed the chair back where he thought it might have been. "I got to go," he said. "See you tomorrow."

She heard him clumping down the stairs, his hand slapping the bannister, and she leaned back into the pillow, the wild daisies across her chest and the petals feathering on her skin. The back door slammed and the house became as quiet and peaceful as her own resting body. She was going to be all right.

CONVALESCENCE DAYS were ice-cream days, cold supper nights, afternoons artificially cooled by the fan Casey's grandfather put in her bedroom window to suck out the hot, stuffy air close under the roof and replace it with a stirred warm bit of moving air.

Jane wanted to move her downstairs into their room, but Casey wouldn't leave. She had grown accustomed to her father's room; she liked its starkness, the dreary, empty look she could fill with visions of her own. Lying there, staring at the blank walls, she decorated them with pictures of airplanes, with college pennants, with the miscellaneous collection of memorabilia she had identified on Taylor's walls.

Being in his room made her feel close to her father. She knew she needed that, just as, since her illness, she'd needed to feel close to her mother. She cried when she heard her mother's voice on the phone that first time, her grandmother having already explained about her sickness, how she was on the mend and there was nothing to worry about. Still, bravery shattered when she heard that breathless, anxious voice that was so necessary to her survival. It was her knowledge of need that made her cry, sobs that mixed helplessness with gratitude. Her grandparents, Taylor, her mother— they all formed links in her circle of protection just as her daddy once had. Until this summer, her daddy had been the whole chain, but he couldn't be that again. Now there were other people.

"I'll be all right, Mama," she said, holding back tears.

Chapter Nineteen

"I'm just fine. We're all just fine." Although she felt so fragile, so tentative, almost unattached in a way that only good health could remedy.

"She ought to get back to bed," Jane said into the phone. "Dr. Kemble said she needs to rest in bed for a week and then another week of limited activity."

"You do that," her mother said, glad she had been offered a responsibility in the matter. "You mind your grandmother and the doctor." She sighed. "I wish I could come up there, Casey," she said. "Sometimes I wish I hadn't let you go at all."

"It's all right, Mama," Casey said. "I'm O.K. We just needed different things this summer."

"I guess you're right," her mother said. "But I miss you, Casey."

"I'll go back to bed now," Casey said to her grandmother when she'd hung up.

"I wish you'd stay down here," Jane said. "It's cooler and the bed is better."

"I like Daddy's room," Casey said. "It's just fine."

Jane took the phone from her, put her arms around her shoulders, and started walking her toward the stairs. "You know, Casey, I've always thought of that room as David's, but this summer it's really become yours. There are a lot of summers left for you to stay here if you want to."

"Where're you two off to?" Taylor asked through the screen.

"Casey's going back to bed," Jane said.

"Oh, no she's not." Taylor pushed open the door for them. "A ride in the car won't hurt her a bit. Might even do her good." He swung Casey into his arms before Jane could protest.

In the front seat of the Chevy in her cotton robe, Casey started laughing. "You rescued me, Taylor! I knew somebody would! Where are we going?"

"It's a secret." Taylor was grinning.

They headed toward the lumberyard. "I've been thinking a lot about you lately, you know," Taylor said. "You gave us quite a scare when you were sick. It got me thinking about your daddy, too, more than I usually do. It's been a pretty long time since your daddy and I were close. He's got five years on me, for one thing, and then we took different directions when we grew up. At least, he took a direction. I've just been meandering along." He turned up a little path that ran into the woods bordering the lumberyard.

"Anyhow," he went on, swerving a little to avoid a bump, "I got to thinking about your daddy, about when we were kids, and I remembered something. So I came out here to see if it was still there and it is— at least it's sort of here. It's going to take some imagination on your part to make it right."

"What is it, Taylor?" Casey felt silly with excitement.

He stopped the car. "Wait and see. I'll have to carry you from here. We should have gotten your shoes on."

He lifted her into his arms and skirted the underbrush until they were in a small opening protected by a large maple. "There." He pointed.

She knew what it was. Splintered, ragged gray wood, sagging frame paint blistered to peeling patches, a propeller half gone, nose bent earthward. It was a plane, a boy's plane. A visionary, awkward, beautiful attempt at making a dream come true.

"He built it," Taylor said. "He had a picture from a magazine. A World War I plane, but I don't remember the name of it or what its history was. He got the lumber from the yard, scraps from the saw, the odd piece Daddy couldn't sell. He wanted silk for the wings, I remember that. It was the depression and he couldn't earn any money. Mama finally gave him the summer sheers off the living-room windows, but I don't think she ever came out here and saw it. Daddy, either. Just David and me. He let me help him sometimes, because one kid couldn't do it all. It was fun, but I didn't really understand what it was all about, not until I started fixing up my car. I didn't feel anything that strong when I was a kid, not like your daddy did."

"I want to get in the cockpit," Casey said against his shoulder.

"Lord, Casey, it's rotten. I'm surprised it's standing at all. It's been out here in the weather twenty years. I think it would fall apart completely if you laid a hand on it."

"I have to touch it, though," Casey said. "Don't you see that?"

He was silent, then took her closer to the plane and stood her on her bare feet in the mossy dirt. The wood was damp and soft under her fingers. She touched the fuselage gently, then the rib of the wing where once her grandmother's sheers had been.

"Sometimes I think that he'll never come back," she said. "I imagine what it would be like with just Mama and me, and then I'm so afraid, like thinking will make it happen. So I try not to think about it, but the thought is always there. What if he doesn't come back, I think, before I can stop myself."

"We can't make something bad happen just by think-ing about it," Taylor said. "I know that for sure."

"What about good things? What about wishing Dwayne would like me until he did? And you and Grandma wanting me to get better so much that I did?"

"But you did something about Dwayne liking you. You tried to be the kind of person he liked. And we took care of you when you were sick. We tried to let you know we loved you, even when you were asleep. David wanted to fly, so he built a plane. Of course, it wouldn't fly anywhere but in his head, but that was enough. The important thing was he did something about what he wanted."

"I think he's coming home," Casey said, lifting her arms for Taylor to hold her again. She felt tired, but healthy, too.

"No doubt about it," Taylor said, hugging her. "And you're going to get well. And we're going to the races and I'm going to win until Gwen is up to her neck in trophies!"

"I don't know about that." Casey laughed. "But I feel good already."

• 20 •

Late August. The garden almost in, the last of the tomatoes weighting the spindly vine, wormy and not worth picking. Corn stalks had begun to shrivel, leaves edged with brown, and their yield was tough and had to be scraped off the cob. Only the weeds grew, standing high along the fence around Dwayne's diamond.

The final stretch of heat was smothering, and it didn't go away. Long into the night people walked the streets restlessly, speaking softly to one another across their hedges and from their porches. They watched the night sky hoping for a wind, any slight stir of breeze to dry their sweaty skin and cool the tin roofs of their smoldering houses.

Now and then it rained. Clouds formed magically and big, splashing drops soaked the grass and lawn furniture. But immediately the sun came back out and wilted the newly nourished grass and leaves. After the shower it seemed hotter than before.

Casey and Dwayne took turns deciding what they could do to entertain themselves. About every other turn, Dwayne would suggest they play catch or ride his bike, something he'd forgotten Casey was not yet allowed to do, and she would have to remind him of what the doctor had said about another week of rest, although she felt fine.

So they watched television, played cards, and read comic books. Casey found an old collection of wildlife stories that had belonged to her daddy and she read some of them to Dwayne while he lay on the porch floor, his head on a cushion Jane had provided Casey with in the swing, bare legs stretched out to get the breeze that the moving swing created around her. She read slowly, glancing occasionally at Dwayne's face to see if he was listening or if he was bored. Once he fell alseep, but when she nudged him awake with her foot, he denied his lack of attentiveness and told her what a good story it was.

Once when she was feeling restless and depressed, she told him he should find something better to do than hang around a sick person.

"You want me to go?" he'd asked, ducking his head.

"It's not that," Casey said. "I just don't want you to think you have to sit here with me."

"Next week we'll play ball," Dwayne promised. "We'll go to the races."

She couldn't bring herself to tell him that next week she'd be gone.

The family had talked about it even before she became sick, how she would have to be back home by the first of September when the school term began. Every week her mother reminded her, knowing exactly how many days were left. Her mother missed her during those hours between her two jobs and late at night when she was at home alone, no sleeping child in the house, no bowls left with drying bits of cereal or melted ice cream, no wet swimsuit on the bathroom rug, no one to speak to. She had only her own clutter, her own ironing draped over the chair, her own needs to take care of.

Casey knew there was something to be said for having someone depend on you. She'd learned that from Dwayne. Having responsibility made people responsible. Having someone to love gave you a chance to be loved yourself.

She looked down at Dwayne, his face screwed up in concentration over the words in a comic book. Perhaps once, years ago, her father had sat there with Dwayne beside him, and they had read and dreamed together— dreams of growing up, of adventure, of flight. They had traded secrets and bubblegum cards. They had acknowledged their disdain for girls and their dedication to whatever sport was seasonable.

But then they had grown up. Years that once seemed so endless had one by one fallen away, until now, on a muggy afternoon in August, they were miles apart, separated by some genetic mystery that was as unconquerable as Babe Ruth's home run record.

Casey had taken her father's place with Dwayne. She could see that now, how the pattern had repeated itself. And she could see how she would have to leave him, too.

She would grow up. By next summer she would be different. Already she felt the changes for which she had no words, no explanation that could make him understand how deep inside, where both her fever and her coolness had so recently been, there was a throbbing sense of life just waiting for a winter's nour-ishing. She would never be the same.

But Dwayne would. Next summer and the next. Then on and on until she was grown and maybe had chil-dren of her own. Dwayne would be the same. Oh, his hair would probably begin to gray, his eyes weaken as he squinted from the mound into the afternoon sun. He would stop playing baseball every day, and gradually his field would grow up, weeds choking home plate. He would lose the hard, quick agility of his body slowly and then loosen his belt a notch, sur-prised by the appearance of fat around his middle. He would sense the passage of time but never put his finger on it. He would grow old without ever having been a young man or a middle-aged man. Without the moments that are intended to get him ready for old age.

"Dwayne, let's go somewhere," she said suddenly.

He looked up frowning, the comic-book images still clouding his mind. Then her invitation registered and he was up like a shot, slapping his thighs and grinning at her. "You mean you got well? You mean we can do something!" And he bounded across the street to get his bike.

They would ride downtown, Casey thought. She would perch on the back fender, feet lifted away from the spokes, hands clutching the seat springs. Dwayne would pump, gathering speed against the burden of her added weight, and then they would coast, shirts blowing, eyes half-closed in the hot breeze.

The deserted streets would lay open like uncharted terrain, houses would be swallowed up by thick, steamy jungles. They would be sailing, soaring; there would be nothing to call them back. No warnings of the years to come. No reminders of the past. No hollow laughing voice to call a man a boy.

It was not, Jane Flanagan told Pansy, expected to be a happy occasion, but she had nevertheless told Taylor to bring Gwen and now she was inviting Pansy and Hazard to come for a farewell supper for Casey.

"I don't think I can stand to see her go," Jane said in Pansy's kitchen.

Pansy was dicing potatoes for a salad. She dug out the eyes carefully, swished the pared potato under the faucet, and chopped it with quick, efficient motions into the pan of water. The water turned milky.

"She's like my own child," Jane continued. "I always wanted a little girl, you know. I kept hoping for a third child, but—oh, well, we should be grateful for the blessings that do come our way. Two fine sons. A healthy, happy granddaughter," She sighed. "I just hate to think about her going back to Fort Jackson. She'll miss David more, I know that. Sometimes I feel so lucky that I'm still here where he grew up. I'm constantly reminded of him, you know. Every room has its own special memories of him as a boy. I miss him less this way."

"She has memories of him there," Pansy said, rinsing another potato.

"How much salad are you making?" Jane asked, watching it disappear into the pot.

"Enough for Hazard to have some in his lunch tomorrow. He loves cold potato salad in his lunch." Pansy smiled, glad she knew that about him. Every day there was something new to learn. It seemed strange to her and at the same time delightful that after all those years there still remained meaningful, daily habits to learn about him.

"So you'll come to supper?" Jane asked, returning to her original subject.

"Of course we will. It sounds like a lovely way to thank Casey for the summer. She's meant a lot to Hazard and me, you know. It's been good being around young people. They don't seem as confused about life as the rest of us, although I suppose they are. I'm just grateful that I don't feel so confused anymore." Pansy set the pot of potatoes on a burner and adjusted the flame.

"You're happy, aren't you?" Jane said.

"I don't think about happiness," Pansy said. "It seems like such an extraordinary sensation. I'm content, though. I feel loved. It's what I've always envied about you, Jane. You show love so clearly, I've always thought. It's so unadorned in you, so unencumbered by questions of degree or worth. It simply *is*. Now I think I feel that too."

"We've come a long way together, Pansy," Jane said, going to hug her.

"Tomorrow night, then," Jane said. "To say good-bye to Casey."

"Yes." Pansy smiled. "She'll be back, Jane. Surely the war will be over by next summer and David will be home. They'll all come. We have that to look forward to."

So the next evening they assembled in the Flanagan's dining room, everybody in their old places. They had all dressed up a little for the occasion. Pansy wore a new dress from her unused trousseau, and Hazard wore a pale blue shirt she had bought for him. Gwen was wearing a cool summer dress, but it had little capped sleeves and a touch of lace that made her look as innocent and wholesome as it did youthful.

Casey wore pants. Her only dress, the blue wedding eyelet, hung in the closet upstairs, never to be worn again. But her hair had grown over the summer and it framed her face softly, curling a little against her cheekbones. Maybe she would let it grow over the winter.

Supper was quiet. Between bites, someone would remind them of how quickly time went and they would agree. The summer had certainly gone quickly. They hoped the same of the winter.

Jane dreaded the winter, she said. She hoped it didn't ice up like it did last year. She recounted broken bones in the neighborhood. Ben recalled a snow from his childhood that stayed on the ground two months, turning yellowish, then brown, disfiguring the farmland almost until spring. They all hoped it would snow only once, a big fluffy snow that would last two or three days and could be easily cleared from the streets.

Gwen spoke up, shyly at first, as if this were her first time at their table, but then more boldly as her excitement grew. She was quitting her job at the five and dime and had enrolled in a secretarial course. She beamed at them, and Taylor took her hand openly and held it at the table. Casey thought they looked like two people with one future between them.

When the meal was over, Gwen followed Casey into the kitchen.

"We'll do them," they said to Jane and Pansy, who

were already putting aprons on to do the dishes. "We want to."

So Jane and Pansy left them to it and went into the living room where Hazard was fingering at the old upright piano Jane had owned since David and Taylor were in grade school.

"We should have a glass of wine," Jane said. "Wouldn't that be nice?"

"I have some homemade," Pansy said, remembering a bottle given her by a neighbor the previous autumn. "It's in the pantry, Hazard."

By the time the girls were finished in the kitchen, Hazard had returned with the bottle and Jane had dusted out the seldom-used wine goblets from the breakfront. Ben poured out the dark sweet wine and they sipped it eagerly and then smiled at each other.

"It's good," Taylor said.

"It's fine," they all agreed.

Jane put a record on the phonograph. They sat around the room, their glasses loose in relaxing fingers, and were silent, smiling at each other. They would miss Casey, but next summer she would be back. David would be back. Life went on.

Hazard stirred a little. The music had swept over him like a scent from his past that conjured up his best memories—places, times when he had abandoned himself to his mood and felt completely free.

"Casey, sing us a song," he said.

Casey felt the sudden flood of embarrassment she always felt, but then, looking around the room, she couldn't help but want to give them something, some gift that only she had to give. She remembered Hazard that first day when he'd come into her room, how he'd let her talk and how when she'd finished, she hadn't felt so out of place anymore. She remembered her grandmother's face when she'd stepped off the bus and her grandfather's tone when he'd tried to talk to her about Dwayne. She remembered Taylor teaching her to drive and Gwen's moment of truth on a sandy beach blanket. She remembered Pansy's quiet glow the night Hazard proposed. The hours spun into her head, as soft and warm as the wine on her stomach.

"I'll play," Jane said and went to the piano.

Casey flipped through the worn sheet music for a moment, then picked one out and put it on the stand.

"*It had to be you,*" she sang softly, looking at each of them in turn, her hand resting on her grandmother's shoulder. "*It had to be you . . . I wandered around and fin-al-ly found, some-body who —*" She smiled at Hazard. "*Could make me feel true . . . Could make me feel blue . . . And even be glad, just to be sad, thinking of you.*"

Hazard was patting his foot lightly. From his side, Pansy could feel the rhythm pulling at him, the urgency he felt to move his limbs in that graceful, yet somehow awkward, way of his.

"Hazard, dance," she said softly. "Dance."

He heard her over the trill of the piano, but at first he didn't believe it. It was too much for him to expect, too much to ask for. He felt her touching his arm, fingers easing him up so he found himself in front of her. He knew he was grinning foolishly but he couldn't help it.

"*Some others I've seen,*" Casey sang, "*Might never be mean . . . Might never be cross or try to be boss . . . But they wouldn't do . . .*"

"Dance." Hazard read the silent word form on Pansy's lips.

He moved his feet obediently, spinning on his toes, arms loose. The music from the old piano was like an orchestra. Casey's voice was Judy Garland's. And he, for the first and only time in his life, was Fred Astaire. And so he circled the room, hearing with every note and seeing on every face, the acknowledgment of Pansy's touching, final acceptance of him. She loved a dancing man.

THEY ALL went to the bus station. It was almost noon, so Taylor, Ben, and Hazard shut down the lumberyard before the whistle blew and came down to find Pansy, Gwen, and Jane already there with Casey and Dwayne in tow. Dwayne had lugged the suitcase, they said. He grinned at the men, proud of having been useful.

"It was heavy, too," he said to Taylor. "She's got bricks in there."

"No bricks," Casey said. "I've got my baseball glove, though."

"Don't you forget it next summer," Dwayne said. "We got to play baseball."

The bus roared into the station.

"Here it is," Hazard said. He had tears in his eyes. "We're going to miss you, Casey," he said, hugging her shoulder.

"We certainly are," Pansy added, patting her from the other side.

The three of them stood staring at the bus as the

door opened and the driver got off to load the new passenger's baggage.

"You've got those sandwiches, don't you?" Jane asked anxiously.

"And that candy to snack on," Gwen added. "It's my last day at the candy counter, so I thought you should get to try everything."

"You change buses once," Taylor said, studying Casey's ticket. "You'll know where, because this bus ends its run there. You'll have a few minutes. Time to get a drink and go to the bathroom."

"She got here just fine," Ben said, hugging her. "She can get home just fine, too, can't you, Casey?"

The baggage loaded, the driver slammed the compartment door shut.

"It's time," Casey said. She felt weak, like she was sick again.

They each hugged her once more, everyone except Dwayne, who stood a little to the side just watching, as if he were studying how to say good-bye.

"Well," they all sighed.

Casey stepped away from them toward the bus.

"Hey boy," a voice said behind her, just like she'd hoped it would.

"Hey Dwayne," she said softly, turning to the man who wore a stained cap low over his forehead and carried, bulging from his side pocket, a baseball. "Listen," she said, hearing tears in her voice. "You take care, you hear?"

"Next summer—" he started, then he stopped. He pulled out his handkerchief and wiped his eyes brusquely. "Oh, shoot."

"We'll all be here," Jane said.

"Yeah," Dwayne said, grateful she had rescued him from his bumbling. He smiled and opened his arms like he'd seen Taylor do.

"I love you, Casey," he said, hugging her hard.

She felt that body close for the first time, felt the power in his back and arms as he swung her off her feet against his chest. He would survive. She knew that now. All these people who loved him would help. She would help. But mostly he would survive because what he saw of life was so often good, and because he was willing to forgive what wasn't.

"I love you, too," she said.

THE LANDSCAPE changed. First the rows of houses fell away to scattered ones set in the middle of dried-up tobacco and corn fields. Then there were the woods, tall dark stands of narrow pines, their floors deep and brown with needles. Then the flat land, the endless miles spreading out before them, hot and silent.

Casey closed her eyes. The bus hummed its rolling rhythm. But what she heard was the metallic clang of a baseball against an empty oil drum. What she saw was a distant figure on a mound, his cap pulled low above his working jaw as he swung both hands high over his head, pushed off his left foot onto his right, swung his left leg into the air, dropped his right arm behind his back, brought it around to let the ball fly, wham into the drum.

"It's a hit!" a voice yelled in her head. "Hey boy, you see that? It's a hit!"